VULPES THE RED FOX

Vulpes caught the scent of the trappers coming across the field that bordered the woods. He bolted to cover. A short distance away he met his father. The old fox had come to help his son as he had so many times in the past. But the chain was strong and there was nothing he could do. With the approach of the trappers they knew they must flee.

They dashed away together and did not stop until they reached an open spot on the crest of a hill far away....

The old fox glanced at his son. Vulpes had outgrown his protection. He was no longer an unschooled pup. He had proven himself on the hunt. He stood quietly before him with the assurance of the experienced fox.

Then the old fox turned and glided into the woods. Soon he disappeared in the growing dusk. Vulpes stood fast, realizing he would never see his father again. The gathering darkness enveloped him. He was alone.

OTHER PUFFIN BOOKS YOU MAY ENJOY

Vulpes the Red Fox

VULPES
THE RED FOX

Jean Craighead George
and John George

Illustrated by Jean Craighead George

PUFFIN BOOKS

PUFFIN BOOKS
Published by the Penguin Group
Penguin Books USA Inc., 375 Hudson Street, New York, New York 10014, U.S.A.
Penguin Books Ltd, 27 Wrights Lane, London W8 5TZ, England
Penguin Books Australia Ltd, Ringwood, Victoria, Australia
Penguin Books Canada Ltd, 10 Alcorn Avenue, Toronto, Ontario, Canada M4V 3B2
Penguin Books (N.Z.) Ltd, 182-190 Wairau Road, Auckland 10, New Zealand

Penguin Books Ltd, Registered Offices: Harmondsworth, Middlesex, England

First published in the United States of America in 1948 by
E.P. Dutton, a division of Penguin Books USA Inc.
Published in Puffin Books, 1996

12 13 14 15 16 17 18 19 20

LIBRARY OF CONGRESS CATALOGING-IN-PUBLICATION DATA
to come

Printed in the United States of America

VULPES THE RED FOX

CHAPTER ONE

Vulpes, the Red Fox, was born in a den in Maryland. It was April. The snow had gone. The woods were cold and wet. A chill rain splashed through the barren woodlands and filled the earth till it could hold no more. In the uplands the rising streams raced along their twisting beds. The river bottomlands of the Potomac swirled with muddy flood waters. Winter lingered in the cold.

In the warmth of the den spring had come. Seven foxes were born. They lay huddled against their mother's breast deep in the dark den. Their eyes were sealed. Their first want was the milk of their mother. When their hunger was satisfied the foxes dropped off to sleep. This was their life for nine days.

Vulpes knew his brothers and sisters only as

whimpering cries and warm bodies that tumbled and shoved and kicked against him. He felt the cold wet nose of his mother nuzzling him, and the moist tingle of her tongue caressing him.

Then one day in the middle of April, Vulpes became aware of something new. There were dim blurred figures that accompanied the kicks and squirms. His mother's cold wet nose was black. Beyond the soft white fur of her breast there was a

dim glow from the outside world. Vulpes could see.

He looked at all his brothers and sisters. They were gray and round. It seemed to Vulpes there were a lot of them. He looked up. His mother was looking down at him through her yellow slanting eyes. Except for the dim light at the end of the tunnel Vulpes thought this must be the whole world.

With this settled, he tumbled back to his mother's breast.

Outside the den, the red maples had burst into bloom. The brooks were lined with the yellow-green flowers of the spice bush.

The days went on and Vulpes became more and more curious about the light at the end of his world. He sat and watched it for hours at a time. It was bright and wonderful. Presently he discovered that the light changed. Sometimes it was gone for a long time. This was night. Sometimes it was gray. This was rain. Sometimes it was blacked out for a short time. At these times Vulpes caught a new smell in the musky den. He sensed another presence. This was his father bringing food to his mother.

Vulpes wondered where his father went in the light. It puzzled him. He felt he must know.

Then one day his mother darkened the tunnel and disappeared as his father had done. The little fox felt alone. The rounded den seemed large and empty. He huddled close to his brothers and sisters. They all whimpered complainingly.

When his loneliness became too great, he left his noisy kin to find his mother. He waddled down the tunnel. The light became brighter and brighter. Suddenly there was a second light. He turned his head and peered down another long tunnel. This confused the little fox. He turned to run for the safety of the darkness behind him. Before he had reached it, he felt himself being picked up by his mother. She carried him down the tunnel into the blinding light of the outside world. It was the end of April.

Vulpes found himself in what he believed was a den, a den that was huge and shining. The light was all around. One part of it was so bright he couldn't look at it. This was the sun. It was warm and pleasant. This den was so large that Vulpes could not see the end of it. This *was* the world.

The young pup scrambled unsteadily to a nearby stone. He wanted to see more of this colorful world. The spring woods abounded with color. The red keys of the maples dangled above him. A loose swirl of Virginia bluebells surrounded him, and the yellows and greens of the dog-tooth violets swept the hill below him. At the foot of the hill the old Chesapeake and Ohio Canal was fringed with the

fresh greens of the willows. The willows stretched beyond the canal to the brown flood waters of the Potomac. The lacy rush of the river hung over all.

As he watched the colors of spring, Vulpes caught the movement of his shadow beneath him on the rock. As he moved, it moved with him. He looked at it. Slowly Vulpes reached out for it. Slowly the shadow reached back. As he took his paw away, the shadow did the same. Whatever he did, the shadow followed. The fuzzy outline fascinated the little fox. He ran with it. He pounced on it, and finally he lost it behind a tree. He stuck his nose out to see if it was on the other side of the tree. And there, below him, was the shadow, sticking its nose out.

He was about to spring on it when a movement at the mouth of the den caught his eye. A venturesome brother had followed him into the sunlight. Vulpes ran over and nipped him on the foot. The two foxes rolled in a mock skirmish. They found their voices in melodious "wurps" as they tumbled over and over in a cluster of pale spring beauties.

Suddenly a bolt of blue came screaming through the blossoming redbud trees overhead. Vulpes and

his brother looked up to see a pair of meddlesome blue jays. They glanced toward their mother. She was calm and undisturbed. Her poise reassured them and they went back to their play.

The young foxes played on until evening. With the lengthening of the shadows came the last carol of the birds. The whistling note of the cardinal rose clear and sweet above the crystal melodies of the wood thrushes. Near the den a flurry of leaves marked the spot where a red-eyed towhee was still scratching vigorously in the wood bottoms. His sharp "Chewink" rang out through the woods. There was the plaintive wavering melody of the white-throated sparrows as they sang, "Old Sam Peabody, Peabody, Peabody, Peabody." And the "Whicherty, whicherty, whicherty," of the Maryland yellow-throats along the wet brush lands bordering the canal echoed through the bottoms.

The long hours of play had tired the little foxes and they were glad to go to bed with the birds.

As the days went by the seven pups spent more and more time playing around the den. The den was hidden in a rocky slope on the north side of the canal bank where it got the warm southern sunlight. Built long ago and now abandoned, the canal made an ideal homeland for the fox. The den was first used by an old woodchuck. Several years ago Vulpes' parents had found it and enlarged it for their own use. Back from the small rocky entrances they dug long tunnels. At the end of them they scooped out two hollows. One was where Vulpes was born, in the other his parents sometimes stored food.

Uphill from the den the hills rolled back to the distant farmlands. Sometimes Vulpes and his brothers and sisters romped in the woods behind the den. They would chase one another around the tree trunks and explore the animal trails in the spring woods.

Vulpes loved to smell the new odors he found: the chipmunks, the squirrels and the white-footed mice. Every time he caught a new scent he would bounce over to his mother and ask her who smelt like that. She would tell him who it was.

Then one afternoon Vulpes smelt an animal that was like nothing else in the woods. He looked to his mother and was alarmed to find her chasing the cubs into the den. She flashed to Vulpes' side, picked him up by the scruff of the neck and carried him off, as the voices of two boys sounded through the woods.

His father darted past him to a hiding place over the canal. Here in the tall grasses he could watch the boys without being seen. The old dog fox saw them go up the tow-path on the other side of the canal. They were carrying fishing rods on their shoulders, and would laugh and shout as they skipped stones over the water.

Presently his father came back to the den and stood before his wobbly son. This was Vulpes' first experience with man. His father warned him that this was his most dangerous enemy. With this the old fox turned around and trotted swiftly away.

Vulpes sat back on his haunches and thought of what his father had warned. Who were these animals that this great hunter feared? He decided to see for himself. He stuck his nose out of the den and sniffed the air. Then, with one eye showing around the edge of the rock, he peered down the old tow-path. Vulpes was startled to see that they walked on two feet like the birds. Surely, anything as dangerous as that would have four legs like his father, not just two like the gentle warblers and the perky towhees. He had seen his father stalk and spring upon birds; surely, he could do the very same with men.

Vulpes was thinking very hard about these new animals when a yellow butterfly came gliding past his nose. He forgot the boys, who were now out of sight. Happily the little fox ran out into the sunlight after the butterfly. Without making a sound he leapt at the flitting insect. He chased it down the rocky bank to the water and was disappointed when the pretty little insect flitted over the canal and down the hill toward the river. Vulpes looked at the water's edge to see if he could cross and continue his chase. He put his left foot down and found it was wet and very unsafe. The ripples he made pleased him. He barked at them as they rolled away and knocked against the old dried stems of the cattails. He soon forgot the butterfly and was busy splashing his foot in the water.

The little fox yapped at a last ripple. Then he looked up at the evening sky. He was watching the colors of the fading sunset when a steady "Urp, urp, urp, urp" in the cattails frightened him. He instinctively fell into a crouch, his head turned to one side, his ears pointed forward. From a patch of arrowhead in the swampy bottom of the canal a second voice answered the first. Then a third rose from a patch of pond lilies. Vulpes looked from the cattails to the arrowheads to the pond lilies. He saw nothing. Other "urps" added to the growing din. He stared at the singing water. As he watched, he heard another voice. It whistled meekly, "Pe-ep, pe-ep, pe-ep, pe-ep." The noise grew louder. It drowned out the roar of the river in the distance.

Spotted here and there through the swampy bottom a series of "erderps" rang out. More and more

voices joined the chorus until the canal bed resounded with ear-splitting songs. Never had Vulpes
heard so much noise. It hurt his ears to listen.

While he stood silently watching, a little ripple
caught his attention. Floating on the water was a
swamp cricket frog. As its throat swelled up and it
began to sing, Vulpes saw where the "erderps" came
from. He marveled that so tiny a creature could
make so much noise. It was about as big as the petal
on the bloodroot.

On a floating twig beneath him he found Hyla,

the spring peeper. He thought Hyla would burst, his throat swelled so as he uttered his shrill "Pe-ep."

Suddenly Vulpes realized that Pipiens, the leopard frog, had been sitting not two feet away from him all this time, but because of his black-spotted green back, the little fox thought he was an old stick in the swamp. Pipiens blended well with the dark waters blotched with green leaves.

All at once the frogs stopped. In the sudden silence that followed Vulpes heard the boys returning from the river, laughing and talking as they ran along the canal.

"Hey, look, a young fox!" one of them shouted to the other. "Let's catch him."

"We can cross to his side on those rocks," the other called back.

As the boys hurried down across the rocks, the frightened Vulpes, remembering what his father had said, scampered to a deep crevasse along the bank. He crawled as far back as he could go. Trembling, he waited.

He heard the boys calling excitedly beneath him.

"Where did he go?"

"Must have gone up in those rocks somewhere," the other answered.

Vulpes was surprised that they could not find him. He learned his most dangerous enemy could not smell.

It wasn't long before Vulpes heard the chorus of the frogs start up again. The boys had given up their search and tramped away.

He slipped cautiously from his hiding place as his mother came gliding over the rocks toward him. She had come to bring her frightened pup home. He scampered up the hill before her and tumbled into the den.

CHAPTER TWO

Vulpes loved the evenings around his den. Early spring nights on the Potomac River were full of sound and activity. He liked to listen to the sweet liquid tones of the woodlands, and feel the cool winds that came in from the water. The call of the whip-poor-wills floated through the lonely hills. He heard the courting woodcock on the grassy knoll above the den. He listened to its twittering flight song as the bird spiraled high into the air. Along the bottoms he heard the nasal squawk of the black-crowned night heron above the chorus of the frogs.

On one of these nights young Vulpes heard the deep resonant voice of Bubo, the great horned owl. Bubo boomed out, "Whoo, whoo, whoo-oo, whoo, whoo." Bubo was the tiger of the woodland

birds and his voice sent a shudder through all who
heard it.

These nights Vulpes began to appreciate the
tragedy that hung over the woodland creatures at
all times. They must be constantly alert. Down in
the dark waters of the canal many hunters preyed
upon the frogs. Beneath the surface lurked the bass,

who came up to take the frogs with an angry swirl.

Nycticorax, the black-crowned night heron, waded in the shallows of the canal. After several deliberate steps on his long thin legs, Nycticorax would freeze motionless. He looked very much like a stick jutting out of the black waters. Then there would be a sudden thrust of his long spear-like beak. Another frog was gone.

As the bass retreated to his underwater lair beneath the log when Nycticorax came, so the night heron flew up the canal on the approach of Vison, the mink.

While the young foxes were playing in the night, their mother was ever on guard. She knew that her youngsters were not safe from Vison or Bubo, for they were inexperienced in the ways of the wild. She never let them get too far away from her sight. She was the first to catch the scent of Vison as he came to the canal to hunt, and she was the first to twitch her ears at the faint far-away bark of the dogs. She let the seven little foxes romp and tumble close to the den, but when they went exploring she followed their movements closely. She left them only to hunt for food for herself, and when she was gone, her mate was close by to protect them from the constant dangers.

One night Vulpes and his brothers and sisters

were frolicking before the den on the fresh spring carpet. It was great sport for the young foxes to pounce upon their mother's twitching tail. They would crouch behind a stone with youthful boldness. Then they would dart on unsteady legs to sink their tiny teeth in her big, brushy tail. With an easy flick of her brush, their mother would bowl them over. The young pups would stumble to their feet and rush back with renewed fury, yapping and barking happily.

Watching them from the earth where she was stretched languidly, their mother knew the seven little foxes would soon be able to hunt. Their sense of timing was becoming sharper and sharper. More often they caught her tail now than missed.

Rolling back from a brisk swish of his mother's tail, Vulpes sprawled onto the hard back of a box turtle. He stuck his nose down to find its head and was amazed to discover it had none. Vulpes felt brave before this headless creature and he barked at it energetically. Then slowly the old turtle house opened. An ugly wrinkled head turned to look at the little fox. Vulpes jumped back as the turtle hissed at him and snapped back into his box. The excited pup made so much noise over the turtle that he attracted his venturesome brother who came rolling down the slope to join the fun.

Meanwhile, across the canal and down the steep bank by the river, a shadow sat on the stub of an old basswood tree. Long ago the basswood had been shattered by a bolt of lightning and now it stood, gray and weathered, in the wet valley by the river. Its jagged top reached almost forty feet into the air. Here in a black hollow of this tree, Bubo, the great horned owl, had made his home. Bubo's spring fam-

ily was almost full grown and ready to leave the
nest. The old owl was out hunting almost all the
time to satisfy the ravenous appetites of his two
owlets.

Bubo shoved off from his post on the basswood
tree in muffled silence and took his perch on an old
sycamore growing along the canal. From the white

bare limbs of the gigantic tree he could watch the beaten trail along the tow-path for the least movement. His sharp ears caught the rustle of a mouse gnawing seeds along the bank. He spread his wings and dropped low along the path. His swift silent flight carried him over the trail. As he neared his victim he shot his legs out before him. His long sharp talons spread out in the four directions of the compass. He struck the mouse.

Bubo was a frightening sight with his great eyes blinking and his bill snapping viciously. His half-extended wings drooped over the grass. In an instant he was off to the basswood tree to feed his hungry young. The mouse was a small meal for such large children. Bubo knew it would do for only one. No sooner had he thrust it into the mouth of a white, fluffy daughter than he was off to the canal to hunt for more.

He studied the canal bed a moment and then crossed to the other side. There he dropped into a slender tulip poplar tree and sat motionless. His black form looked threatening against the night sky. Two great feathered tufts stood up like ears on his round head. His yellow eyes gleamed in the night.

Immediately he caught the barks of the young foxes. He flew closer. From a perch on the edge of a small clearing just below the den he saw Vulpes and his venturesome brother playing with the box turtle.

Silently the owl watched the scene below him. He saw that the two young foxes were alone. Savage as Bubo was, he usually did not bother foxes. However, tonight he must have food. The pups were young. Swift and tireless as she was, their busy mother could not be with all the wandering pups at any one time. The owl well knew the strength of his own sharp talons. He leaned forward eagerly.

The young foxes were unaware of the threat above them. Yet some instinct within Vulpes struck a warning note. He crouched along a greenbrier thicket. In a moment he would have rejoined his venturesome brother who had the turtle on its back. But in that moment the owl struck!

Like a bolt of feathered lightning, Bubo dove past Vulpes. His venturesome brother took the full impact of the attack. A brief, silent struggle followed the dull thud of the strike. Vulpes recoiled into the thicket.

There was a sharp snap of teeth, as Bubo rose heavily with the little fox. With a snarl, Vulpes' mother had flashed to the scene and had leapt at the owl to save her son. An instant too late, her teeth closed on the empty air. Tense and trembling she watched Bubo lift his burden low over the tree tops and disappear.

Sadly she turned to the whimpering Vulpes. She looked long at her frightened son. The great tragedy struck her heart and she called sadly into the night. She turned once more to look at the trees over which Bubo had flown. Then she nudged Vulpes and he scampered out of the greenbrier patch and up the slope to the den. The little fox darted into the dark tunnel without looking back. The five other puppies followed him in when they sensed the fear and grief in their mother's anxious movements.

Over the hill Vulpes heard his father growl at the unseen dangers that forever lurked in the woods.

CHAPTER THREE

May came to the Maryland woods and opened the purple blossoms of the pawpaw. The May-apples bloomed under their green umbrellas, and the Jack-in-the-pulpits stood straight and tall in their green parishes. The floor of the woods was splashed with spring flowers and the warblers flew in from the South. Some stayed to nest, others paused briefly during the day, then resumed their flight northward with the setting of the sun.

The woods along the river were filled with birds. Vulpes felt the happiness of their brilliant songs and rollicked and played in the fresh spring air.

With the coming of June the pups were about half grown. They still lacked the red luster of their parents' coats, but Vulpes could feel a growing strength in his body. As each day passed, he gained more of

the smooth easy grace of his mother and father. He liked to run over the rocks and stretch his young, lithe legs in a race with his brothers and sisters. His explorations became wider and wider until he knew who was nesting in the honeysuckle thickets and who was nesting in the redbud trees all around the den.

More and more of late his father had been dropping mice in the woods near the den. Earlier his father had brought mice right up to their home. But now he was encouraging his young family to seek them in the woods. In this way the little foxes were taught to hunt their food.

One evening Vulpes climbed up to the grassy knoll where the woodcock danced earlier in the spring. He had learned that this was where his father liked to rest. He sat down on a flat rock much as his father had done. From the rock he could see over the canal bank and out to the gorge of the Potomac River. He could look up and down the towpath. He could look through the open woods and see the shrubby fence rows of the farmlands in the distance. The fence rows were twisted with honeysuckle vines that filled the air with a heavy sweet scent.

As he glanced about, Vulpes caught a blur of movement in the woods below him. He studied the movement carefully. Then he wagged his tail, for he saw it was his father. The old dog fox came up to the clearing and gazed at his son. He was surprised to find him there on his high rock. For a moment he stood and looked at him proudly, then he trotted off to join his mate at the den.

Vulpes thought his father might have hidden a mouse while he paused at the edge of the clearing. So he dashed over to the spot. He sniffed the air, and sure enough, he caught the scent of a mouse. Instinctively he hunted. The scent seemed to be coming from a dense clump of grass. He pounced upon it. Quickly he bit down into the tangled mat. At the same time he heard a squeak. Vulpes had caught his first mouse alone!

It was the best mouse he had ever eaten. As he finished he looked up to see his father standing beside him. The old fox was there on his first triumph.

With the coming of July, Vulpes had learned to hunt quite well. July along the Potomac was hot and moist and the little foxes stayed in the cool den during the day. Outside they could hear the heavy drone of insects in the hot summer sun. The birds seldom sang during the day. Only the monotonous call of the vireos and the flycatchers sounded through the woods.

In the cool of the evening Vulpes wandered off through the woods. The summer foliage made heavy shadows along his favorite trail that led to the crest of the hill. He had grown confident—perhaps too confident of his ability as a hunter.

This evening he was out to hunt. He trotted to the grassy knoll where he had caught his first mouse. Often he had caught crickets there and chased rabbits. As he came up over the ridge of the hill he sniffed the air. He smelt nothing in the hot summer evening. He crouched and listened.

Except for the crickets, the hill was silent. This evening he found the crickets of little interest so he trotted over to the fence row that bordered the farmlands. He knew that the shrubby fence rows where the woods met the fields were used as pathways for larger game.

Vulpes looked at the old weathered chestnut rails. They were wound with trumpet vines and honeysuckle that had grown up during the years. Twisted thickets of greenbrier and blackberries stretched along the woodland border. The wildlife found these fences to their liking. There was an abundance of food and at the same time there were many excellent hiding places nearby. They could scurry to cover at the threat of danger.

So it was that these places were used as woodland avenues. Here the quail moved from one feeding patch to another; coons followed the paths to woodland streams; opossums and rabbits, chipmunks and squirrels constantly passed along them.

Vulpes crept through the trumpet vines and honeysuckle and crouched under a fence rail where he could watch the avenues. Presently he saw a rabbit hopping along slowly. Its small nose wriggled as it smelt the new leaves and chewed the tender clover. Vulpes balanced himself for a spring. He scarcely stirred a leaf. When the rabbit was within reach, the little fox flashed out of his hiding place under the rail. He had misjudged. The rabbit burst into a gallop, with Vulpes after him losing ground rapidly. He was no match for the cottontail. But he enjoyed the chase, and followed him out through the field, over the hills and back to the woods.

It wasn't long before the rabbit was out of sight. Now Vulpes was following him by scent alone. Gradually the trail became weaker and weaker. Then he lost it.

Vulpes sat down and scratched his head with his hind foot. He sniffed the air. Presently he saw what his nose had been expecting. A chipmunk was scurrying down the side of a gnarled ironwood tree.

The chipmunk looked up from his busy work and glanced at Vulpes. He came lower and flicked his tail, teasing the little fox into a chase. Vulpes sensed his play and turned his nose away, ignoring him. But Tamias, the chipmunk, was not to be brushed off when he felt in a frivolous mood. He ran down the ironwood trunk to a crotch about three feet above the ground. He fussed noisily at the fox. Vulpes looked up at the evening sky. Tamias flew down the side of the tree and skidded over to a near-by oak. He buzzed gleefully at the little fox.

This began to excite Vulpes. He waited for the

next move that Tamias should make. Presently, the noisy chipmunk came down the oak to make a dash for the ironwood again. Vulpes pretended he didn't see him. He looked at an oak leaf twisting in the light wind. Tamias whizzed by. Vulpes leapt after him. There was no squeal. Only the scratch of little feet on the ironwood and then a mad chatter from the limb of the tree where Tamias sat in safety.

Vulpes lifted his head into the air and trotted off toward the hill that overlooked the river. Maybe he didn't catch the rabbit, maybe he didn't catch the chipmunk, but he knew where some good crickets and grasshoppers were and he would show them what a fine hunter he was.

Early one morning while Vulpes slept in the den with his nose at the tunnel, he smelt some men coming down the tow-path. His curiosity was aroused and he crept to the end of the tunnel to watch them. They were talking and laughing and their voices rang out clearly in the cool air of the summer morning. Vulpes looked back at his brothers and sisters. They were curled in tight, ruddy balls with their now rather pretentious tails swirled up to their noses. They were almost too big for the den, but they still came back to it to sleep and rest. It was a haven for the little foxes although they were almost full grown. Vulpes' parents rarely slept with the cubs now. They would go out on a bare rock and sleep during the warm daylight hours. However, they were always near-by.

Vulpes saw that everyone was sleeping, but decided he would follow the men. He wanted to discover for himself what made them his greatest enemy. His curiosity was still unsatisfied.

The men had passed the den and were well up the path. Vulpes stepped lightly over the rocks and glided down into the grassy bottom of the canal. The summer had filled the canal with reeds and weeds. The water ran only in a trickle down the bed. The frogs made less noise these hot days, and only occasionally on a cool night did Vulpes hear Hyla.

As he crossed the canal bed and darted up the bank on the other side, a cloud of butterflies flew up before him and scattered like leaves over the water. When Vulpes had passed they settled back to the muddy pools.

As the fox came up on the tow-path he saw that the men had turned off the canal and were following a foot trail down through the woods toward the river. Clinging to the foliage that now almost overgrew the path, Vulpes followed them silently.

He turned down the trail where the men had gone, and followed them just on the other side of a low ridge. They strode through the woods fearlessly and came out to the river at the gorge. From a safe distance Vulpes could watch them. They had no sharp fangs or claws. There was nothing about these smooth, hairless animals that aroused any respect in the little fox. He crept closer, clinging low to the ground and barely turning a twig. He was not afraid, yet he naturally followed the instincts of the wild within him. He remained hidden.

There were three men. They all carried rifles. One of the men raised his gun to his shoulder and pointed it at a log floating in the river. The sharp report surprised the fox. He drew back. His muscles tensed and his ears shot forward. For a moment he felt real fear. The log that the man had shot bobbed in the river. A spray of water burst into the air around it.

Vulpes was about to run, when he saw a second man pointing his gun at a starling. It was digging in a pile of rubbish and driftwood at the water's edge. He sensed the meaning of this and poised alert. The rifle cracked. A wisp of smoke rose from the barrel. Vulpes saw the starling flutter and fall. It was all over in an instant. As the man ran to the spot where the bird lay, the young fox caught the smell of the burnt gunpowder. Vulpes watched another minute, then turned and silently slipped back through the woods. He understood.

As he sped up the hill to the den, he saw his father sleeping on his favorite rock on the knoll. Vulpes paused and looked at him. The old fox lifted his head and exchanged a knowing glance with his son. Vulpes could smell his father's fresh trail that led to the hill. His father had not been there long. He had followed Vulpes to the edge of the gorge and had seen his son and the men.

The old fox flicked his tail. His son had learned one of the most important lessons of his life. He knew how man hunted.

The sun was getting high and the heat was making it uncomfortable to be about. Vulpes climbed to a rock above the den and curled up to sleep for the first time in the open.

As he dozed off, he could hear a red-headed woodpecker pounding at a dead tree above his head. The steady rat-a-tat-tat echoed around the hills of the canal. At first he liked the monotonous hammering. Then he became aware of little pieces of bark dropping around him. He opened one eye. His handsome coat of which he was growing so proud, was peppered with sawdust from the woodpecker's work. Vulpes was annoyed that his first sleep in the open should be marred by this bird. He got up and shook himself. He scowled at the bird in the dead hickory above him. Then he walked down to the den door.

He did not look back to see what his father was doing. He knew that the old fox was watching him in amusement. He crawled down the dark tunnel and fell asleep.

CHAPTER FOUR

With the first frost the woods slowly took on their autumn coloring. The summer green faded out of the leaves and left them gold and red and brown and purple. They decorated the hills along the Potomac and trimmed the fence rows with brilliance. The hickory nuts ripened and fell to the ground. The hazel nuts burst their leafy hulls and popped to the woodland floor. The persimmons ripened and swung like gold bells from the bare limbs of the trees.

Vulpes liked to watch the leaves twist on the twigs, hesitate a moment and then sail off into the wind. When the wind was brisk it sent them cascading down the tow-path in racing swirls.

Tamias, the chipmunk, was busy gathering nuts and acorns for the winter. He would stuff two or

more in his cheek pouches until they were bigger
than his head. Then he would race off to underground storage bins near his burrow. The leaves flew
behind his feet as he scampered wildly through the
autumn leaves.

Down in the canal bottom Vulpes saw the turtles
and frogs digging into the mud to sleep away the
winter. Above them, the brown cattails had burst

into clusters of creamy white seeds that floated along the bottomlands.

Vulpes was a handsome fox. He was taking on the bright burnt-orange luster which gave him the name, Vulpes, the Red Fox. He had few friends. He was not loved by the woodland creatures. Now that he was full grown, he was more than a match for any of the inhabitants of the Maryland woods. He walked alone.

Vulpes seldom saw his parents now. The old foxes had done their job and were encouraging the young foxes to make their way on their own. They

had schooled them in hunting and in wariness and had found them apt pupils. Soon they would sever forever the loose family ties that still held them together.

Already the family had traveled great distances from home. Nevertheless they still liked the river bottoms with their abandoned farms and woodlands. Though they might travel many miles in one day, they were never more than several hours from the den.

On one of his travels Vulpes went to Muddy Branch, a stream about six miles up the canal. He had taken a trail up the river to this wild area along the Potomac. He had crossed over the old canal locks that were rotting in the water. At Great Falls he had listened to the roar of the Potomac River as it rolled over the steep drop in its course. He had passed unpainted and weathered houses where fishermen lived. At last he came to Muddy Branch. The feeder stream had cut a deep and fertile valley as it took its course to the Potomac. On the floor of the valley giant oaks and beech trees spread their ancient limbs over the glossy laurel thickets. This lovely wilderness was the home of many animals. Here there were places where they could find shelter and an abundance of food.

Just above Muddy Branch, at the bottom of a

rolling hill, stood a small farm. Woods surrounded it on three sides, and a narrow rutted road led into it. Corduroy patches along the road marked the springs that opened on the hill and ran down into the wet bottomland below the farm. The bottomland reached out to the river and was tangled with blackberry bushes, greenbrier and honeysuckle. Above the wet thickets rose tall oaks, maples, the river birch and beech trees.

This was the home of old Buck Queen, the fox-hunter. In the backyard stood a model-T Ford. When he wanted to use it he would push it out of the old barn, get in and let it roll down the hill. With a chug, chug, chug of the motor and a couple of bangs, Buck Queen would be bouncing down the rutted road to the main pike.

On Buck Queen's farm there were apples, pears, chickens and turkeys that tempted Vulpes; but there were also dogs. In the kennels which stretched around the house over to the barn and circled the chicken pen were many hunting dogs. These were no pampered house dogs. These were dogs of the fields and streams. There were swift, high-spirited bird dogs, pointers and setters. There were pedigreed champions and blue ribbon winners, dogs that carried away the honors year after year at the field trials. And there were fox hounds.

The fox hounds were smaller and chunkier than the streamlined bird dogs. Though Vulpes did not know it, these hounds had been bred through the years for the specific purpose of hunting him and his kind. Long ago the sportsmen had found that the hounds used for the English fox were far too slow for the swift-footed American fox.

Vulpes had hunted late this night. The eastern sky was growing lighter and long shadows were appearing behind the trees when he curled up on a big stump in a thicket and went to sleep. He was still hungry, for his was a young and ravenous appetite that was hard to satisfy. He thought of the apples in Buck Queen's yard, but remembered the hounds.

After the sun was up a few hours, the far off cry of Brownie, the Red Bone hound, roused him from his light slumber. Vulpes was not the only one to hear the hound. Old Buck Queen was standing along

the road below his farm, listening carefully. At times Buck could spot the hound as he trailed through the wooded bottomlands. The woodsman didn't even have a gun with him this morning. He was just warming up the hounds for the opening hunting season. His old brown coat was open to the sharp weather, and his warm felt hat was pushed back from his forehead. He still held Joe, the Blue Tick hound, on his leash. He was waiting for Brownie to hit a hot trail before he turned the other dog free.

Buck Queen knew his hounds. The young Red Bone would hunt the bottoms close to home. Not flashy, and lacking the initial burst of speed of the Blue Tick hound, Brownie nevertheless had great endurance. He had been known to carry a chase for two days. He never gave up a trail as long as there was one to follow.

The long-spaced yelps of the Red Bone rolled through the thickets. Buck waited until the yelps shortened and became more feverish. This was a fresher trail. He bent down and slipped the leash over Joe's head.

"Go help him, Joe," he said. The Blue Tick hound darted down the road. He cut into the woods above the stream and disappeared in the matted blackberry and honeysuckle thickets.

Presently Buck heard Joe's voice as he joined Brownie on the hunt. Buck started down the road that circled around the foot of the hills. He was heading for a ravine where he knew the foxes often crossed. Buck had spent many years in the woods along the Potomac and had studied the trails the foxes traveled. Some days he would go out with his hounds just to watch the race. The next day he would return with his gun. He would take his station along the fox avenues and wait for them to retrace the route of the day before. In this way he had got many foxes.

As he rounded a bend in the road he met the hounds coming out of the bottoms and heading up the hill. He judged the situation. The fox must be over near his farm. Probably on that hill above the chickenhouse.

Over on the hill, Vulpes knew the hounds were on his trail. He thought of his den far down the river and dropped lightly from the stump and trotted off through the woods.

At the top of the hill he paused. His black ears stood erect on his head as he sniffed the air. The wind was blowing up from the bottomlands and he caught the scent of the hounds and the hunter. For a moment he was frightened. His muscles grew tight and tense as he wondered what to do. Then he bolted down the side of the hill and slipped into the thickets along a stream bed.

This was Vulpes' first hunt. These deep-throated hounds, loose from their kennels and close on his trail, made him uneasy. What did their baying mean? Why did they hunt with such resounding noise? When he went out to hunt he went quietly. Nothing, not even Bubo, could hear him move as he stalked his prey. Procyon, the raccoon, moved silently when he searched the water's edge for food. And Vison, the mink, made no sound as he hunted.

But these hounds were betraying their position with their excited baying. Vulpes knew just where they were. He did not understand such antics.

He sped up the stream bed and crossed another hill. If their baying was a challenge, he would meet it. He knew his own speed. He knew his own cunning. He knew his own endurance. He was certain he could more than hold his own with anything in the woods.

Vulpes was far down the river when he stopped again. He listened. The baying of the hounds sounded faint in the distance. Now he was sure he was far swifter than the dogs, and grew even more confident of his abilities.

He felt his first thrill of the chase. He thought he could lose the hounds any time he wished. So he decided to circle back along the bottoms and encourage the hunt for awhile.

The young fox loped off the hill. He was in no hurry. He would let the dogs gain. Then he would lose them again in the lowlands. He crossed through the woods and skirted the edge of the canal.

He could hear the baying of the hounds grow louder as they closed in upon him. He glanced up the ridge. Through the bare trees he could see them coming. They carried their heads high as they raced along the fresh track.

When Vulpes reached the swamp he turned to follow a ravine. He stopped. There in the brushy valley was Buck Queen. Quickly he sensed the meaning of the baying hounds. They were bringing him to the hunter. Vulpes remembered the men along the river with their guns. In an instant he turned and flashed through the thickets, over the road and straight up the side of a steep hill.

His frightened burst of speed carried him far through the woods. So fast did he run that the hounds were soon well behind him. No longer could he hear them since their voices did not carry out of the valleys. He slowed down. Then, as he topped the summit of a hill, he heard the dogs again. They were following him relentlessly. No distance seemed to discourage them. Though it was easy to put miles between himself and the dogs, they still stuck to his trail with determination. As the hours wore on to noon he wondered if he would ever lose them. Vulpes was worried.

The baying of the hounds had aroused the woods. Vulpes saw a gray fox moving swiftly away from the chase. He skirted the area where one of his brothers had spent the night hunting. His brother was now moving overland to safety.

Though he sped from the hounds, there were other dangers in the woods that even Vulpes did not sense. Beneath a light scattering of earth and leaves, steel traps were planted. Trappers had placed them well. They knew the runways of the fox and at intervals along them they had made their sets. They were baited with food and scents that attracted the fox.

Vulpes' brother moved far ahead of the hunt. On a distant hill he stopped and rested on a rock. He felt at ease. No longer could he hear the baying of the hounds. He stretched out in the autumn sun and licked his fur until it was free and fluffy. Overhead a gray squirrel scolded him. He glanced at the squirrel, got up and trotted to the edge of the woods.

Nearby a trap was set. He caught the scent of its lure. He moved closer. He could smell the rabbit used as bait. Vulpes' brother approached the food. There was a sharp bite of steel on steel. The jaws of the trap closed painfully on his foot, yet the fox did not utter a sound. He carried his hurt silently after the manner of a fox.

Meanwhile Vulpes had been relieved of the chase. When he had seen Buck Queen he had raced across the hills with one idea in mind: to put as much space between himself and the hounds and the hunter as he possibly could. He streaked through the woods like an arrow, moving swiftly and evenly over the hills, down the valleys and out of the area.

As he ran, widening the distance, the hounds slowed down. His trail was becoming fainter and fainter and they were having difficulty finding it in places.

Just about this time Urocyon, the gray fox, who had been aroused by the chase, crossed the hill in the path of the hounds. He was heading for the bottoms. When the hounds came to the spot where Urocyon had crossed Vulpes' trail, they picked up the newer, fresher scent of the gray fox and turned to follow him.

Buck Queen saw the switch from Vulpes to Urocyon. The fox hunter had hurried up the brushy valley with the long swinging strides of the woodsman. From the head of the ravine he had followed the chase by the baying of the hounds. Then he took his post along the side of the trail on the crest of the hill. His quiet erect figure and the mellowed tones of his garments blended smoothly into the woodland scene. He was as much a part of it as the lichen-covered oak behind him. He seemed to stand motionless, yet an easy motion moved his head from side to side. His glance swept across the floor of the open woodland and up and down the trail. It centered for an instant on each flurry of movement he discovered. He saw Urocyon silently thread his way through the trees. The gray fox stopped at the trail

and studied the scene about him much as the woodsman had done. He looked at the now motionless hunter but found nothing to alarm him. Had Buck Queen moved a hand, the fox would have darted for cover. Upwind, there was no telltale scent to reveal the man's presence to the fox. Urocyon moved on into the glade. Then the old hunter saw his laboring Red Bone come baying through the woods and turn to follow the fresh trail of Urocyon. His heart warmed as he heard the tired hound break into full cry on the hot scent.

Vulpes sensed the change in the chase. He eased his pace that had sped him far across the hills. He picked up his brother's trail and followed it leisurely. The exhilaration of the hunt slowly waned, leaving him weary and hungry.

He reached the point where his brother had paused to rest. He was about to curl up on a stump for a nap when the rattle of a chain sent him silently to cover. Then he caught the scent of his brother. He moved forward cautiously. His keen senses were alert. As he reached the edge of the woods he saw his brother in the trap. Nervously he edged closer. His brother clawed the leaves in a frantic effort to free himself. Then Vulpes caught the scent of the trappers coming across the field that bordered the woods. He bolted to cover. A short distance away he met his father. The old fox had come to help his son as he had so many times in the past. But the chain was strong and there was nothing he could do. With the approach of the trappers they knew they must flee.

They dashed away together and did not stop until they reached an open spot on the crest of a hill far away. Vulpes looked at his father. He felt the sadness that gripped his heart. He knew there were things his father could not do.

The old fox glanced at his son. Vulpes had outgrown his protection. He was no longer an unschooled pup. He had proved himself on the hunt. He stood quietly before him with the assurance of the experienced fox.

Then the old fox turned and glided into the woods. Soon he disappeared in the growing dusk. Vulpes stood fast, realizing he would never see his father again. The gathering darkness enveloped him. He was alone.

CHAPTER FIVE

Vulpes began his bachelor winter. The first snows found him well prepared for his rigorous outdoor life. His deep bushy fur with its dense undercoat was as warm and fine as any that could be found in the woodland. As he moved across the winter scene few animals could match the splendor of the colorful picture he made. His fur had taken on the rich lustrous beauty of the blended burnt orange, tawny yellows, ebony black and creamy whites of the mature fox. The golds and red browns of his thick bushy tail were flecked with black. The tip of his tail was white.

He was a magnificent fox. Large for his kind, he was almost three and a half feet long, and weighed over thirteen pounds.

Beneath his fluffy coat the trim lines of his body

lay hidden. His deep chest, narrow waist and bulging thighs were mellowed by the softer contours of his long fur. These hidden lines gave Vulpes the speed and endurance of the fox. His muscles were steeled by his active life, and he covered the woods with a swift, tireless trot.

Vulpes had moved to Muddy Branch. In his evening travels he would frequently sit above the Queen farm, and there on the lonely hill, he would challenge the dogs with his eery squall. The dogs would answer and strain eagerly upon their leashes.

Above the howls of the many dogs, Vulpes would hear Brownie, the Red Bone. And Brownie knew it was Vulpes, the swift-footed red fox that was taunting him. He was anxious to break away and begin the chase.

Now that it was winter, the foxes were scattered and the hunts were going on in earnest. Every few days Vulpes could hear the "hymn" of the hounds as they bayed through the woods in pursuit of one of his kind. On these occasions Vulpes would sit alert, listening to see if Brownie or Joe were on his trail. If several days passed without a challenge, Vulpes would go down to the farm and call to Brownie. Brownie would answer the wild call.

The Red Bone was Vulpes' only friend. The other animals of the woods feared him. The crows screamed when he passed through the fields; the rabbits darted for cover when he came near. Clever and cunning, he lived by his wits and speed, and he lived alone. So it was that the fox was drawn to the one animal that would challenge him and meet him on his own terms.

Brownie was in his prime. He was five years old and was built sturdily in comparison with the slim sleek form of the fox. The hound had been hardened by many hunts. His short hair was reddish brown except for his white belly and black back, and like Vulpes, he had black feet. He had sad brown eyes.

One day when Buck Queen was out hunting with his hounds, Vulpes awoke from a nap to hear Brownie coming down through the hills to Muddy Branch. He wondered if Brownie had found his trail as he waited for him to come nearer. While he waited he saw Urocyon, the gray fox, slip through the trees. Urocyon was smaller and not as swift as Vulpes, but his gray fur blended well with the winter landscape. This made it difficult for the hunters to see him. Vulpes knew that Brownie and Joe had found Urocyon's trail and were after him.

He stood still and watched. The gray fox ran up the side of an uprooted tree and, easily as a cat, came down a big limb to the ground again. He stole off along the edge of the stream and slipped back through the woods behind the dogs.

When Brownie and Joe reached the fallen elm, they lost the trail. In this way Urocyon slowed down the hounds. But Brownie had played this game before. He was not to be deluded so easily. He swung in a circle from the spot where the gray fox had climbed the tree. Joe crossed the creek and with his nose close to the ground, swiftly covered another area. Brownie continued his circle until he hit the creek. Here he picked up the scent and was off through the woods faster than before.

Vulpes was anxious to watch the chase and if possible to join it. He skirted the edge of the hill and followed the baying hounds. Presently he saw the fury of the hunt again. The hounds were not far behind the gray fox. He changed his course and sped into a thicket of greenbrier and tangled honeysuckle. The thicket checked the hounds. Slowly they fought their way through the dense brambles. Meanwhile, Urocyon was through the tangle and zig-zagging through the forest.

Held back by the trap only a few minutes, the hounds burst into a run again and took out after the fox.

Urocyon was beginning to tire. He did not have the endurance of Vulpes. After the race went on to its second hour, he could feel his breath coming in short snaps. Even the slipping leaves under his feet were enemies. The gray fox made a last spurt of energy and leapt into a tree that leaned heavily over a creek. He scuttled up the dark bark. In the first crotch he rested as Joe and Brownie rushed the tree. The dogs leapt at him. They jumped high into the air and clawed the bark in a furious attempt to reach him. Urocyon moved on up. He edged out on a slender limb and looked down at the hounds, panting and wild-eyed.

By the change in the hounds' voices Buck knew they had treed a fox. He knew it was a gray fox for Vulpes and his kin rarely climbed trees. They would stick to the trails and open fields and outrun the dogs. Buck Queen left the road and started up the hill to find the fox.

Vulpes saw the hunter coming. He jumped from a rock hidden in a laurel patch and bounded up the creek. Brownie turned on Vulpes. Like a flash the two darted off through the woods, up the ravine across the creek, over the hill and out to the fields.

Joe paused, glanced at the tired Urocyon, and left for the more vigorous sport—Vulpes.

Joe had hardly left before Urocyon leapt from his perch to the earth. Buck Queen raised his shotgun. The fox was gone. He had glided through the laurel thickets and denned in the rocks. Buck followed him but the game was over. Neither Buck nor his dogs went after a fox in his den.

Far away he could hear Vulpes and the hounds. Vulpes was fresh. No telling how long this would last. He looked up at the sky. It was growing dark and the clouds were heavy. It would probably snow before morning. The old hunter slung his gun through his arm and quietly headed back for the road. He followed it home, prepared some food for Brownie and Joe, set it out and went to bed.

After Vulpes had run for three or four hours and the Maryland countryside was turning dark, he decided to lose the hounds. He remembered the tricks of Urocyon, and ran down to a broad shallow stream about a half mile from the Queen farm. When he had put about three-quarters of a mile between himself and the dogs, Vulpes stepped into the creek and ran through it, following the shallow patches. His trail was lost in the water. Farther up, he stepped out and trotted up to the road. This he followed past Buck Queen's house. For a moment he hesitated, listening. Brownie and Joe had just reached the creek. Their confused voices told the fox they were bewildered and would be some time trying to find his scent in the cold, icy glade. Vulpes turned off the road and went into Buck Queen's yard. Silently he raced across to the apple tree and picked up a frozen fruit. He crossed the yard, slipped under the fence and leisurely climbed the hill with the prize in his mouth. When he reached his favorite resting place in a laurel thicket, he dropped the fruit. It was too old to eat.

It was snowing now. Vulpes curled up on the rock and wrapped his brushy tail around his feet to keep them warm. Meanwhile, below him, Brownie was coming home through the stillness of the snowy night. The hound was tired as he reached the gate and turned into his yard. Somehow he sensed that Vulpes was near, although the falling snow had covered all the trails. He stood still and looked toward the hill. Then he lifted his head and howled into the night.

Vulpes did not answer. He had had enough of a chase for this day. The Red Bone trotted up on the porch and barked. Buck got up and opened the door to welcome his tired hound. He gave him his plate of food, patted him on the head and when he had eaten, took him to his kennel. Brownie fell asleep with his nose out the door. He would find Vulpes in the morning when his tracks would be sharp in the fallen snow.

In a few hours Vulpes awoke and shook the light blanket of snow off his orange-red fur. He stood up and looked into the white woods. Nothing was stirring. The chase had whetted his appetite and he was feeling vigorous and full of life after the short nap.

He liked the snow. It outlined the hills with soft white lines. The trees stood black and delicate against them. The trails were buried and the road lay smooth and clean. Vulpes started off to Muddy Branch where the night hunting was excellent.

As he walked across the snow to find the trail that led to his hunting grounds, Vulpes heard the call of Bubo, the great horned owl. He no longer feared the fierce bird, but he never forgot how the owl had killed his brother. Bubo knew that he was no match for the sly, red fox, and many times was sorry that he ever had bothered the two young brothers, for Vulpes had made him pay for his crime many times over. Vulpes always teased the old owl, by snatching his food away from him when he caught a rabbit or other game too big to carry off, or he would scare his game before he had a chance to strike.

Tonight Vulpes listened to Bubo and snarled softly at him. The old owl heard and stopped booming. He shoved off and flew quietly through the woods. Vulpes watched him. He knew that he would head for the abandoned field where he usually hunted. Tonight with the snow falling, it would probably be difficult for Bubo to find food. Vulpes thought he would make it all the harder. He left the trail he was following, went down the side of the hill, over the road and into the field. Bubo was sitting on the white limb of an old sycamore tree, watching eagerly for some movement in the field. The long clusters of sedge broom that filled the land were bending low with their burden of snowflakes. Vulpes sniffed the air. Bubo would not eat well tonight, he thought.

Just as he was about to run through the field and frighten what prey there might be for Bubo, the wind blew a new sweet scent to him from the other end of the field.

He bounded off to the corner of the field from which the scent came. He moved swiftly and quietly. The fox leapt high over the grasses. Then he froze. Just beyond him seven quail were sleeping. They slept in a small circle with their heads out so that they could keep each other warm. The circle also acted as a fortress. They could watch every direction for enemies. When danger threatened they could burst free, scattering North, East, South and West.

Even though they were roosting in the open field, it would not be easy for Vulpes to catch them for they were nestled down at the roots of the tall dry grasses. Although they slept, any sounds that were foreign to the brush of the night winds would awake the quail. The slightest movement rustled the dried goldenrod and sweet-scented perilla. This sounded an alarm for the birds. With a burr of wings they would be off in the night.

Vulpes inched his way ahead. His erect ears were pointed slightly forward. His quivering nose told him the way. With his keen eyes he searched the darkness. Frequently he stopped and crouched low in the grasses. Then he resumed his stalk. Vulpes did not make a sound. He picked up each foot quietly and carefully. As he put it down he shifted his weight cautiously.

In this way he came within a few feet of the sleeping quail. He gathered his powerful hind feet beneath him and balanced himself for the spring. His flying leap carried him into the midst of the covey.

There was a puff of feathered wings as the quail whirred up into the night. All but one. Vulpes had caught his prey.

As he trotted off with his prize he could hear the other quail calling as they sought each other in the woods and fields. He wondered if Bubo heard their call to assemble. He knew that the old owl would quickly take advantage of the gathering covey. Vulpes thought that perhaps he had done Bubo a favor rather than mischief.

He woke frequently during the night to shake the

snow out of his fur. He would circle around for a few minutes, knocking it to the ground. Then he would settle back on his rock again and doze off. All night the flakes came down over Muddy Branch and the shores of the Potomac River.

When Vulpes awoke in the morning, it was still snowing and the leaves were buried under the whiteness. He got up and stretched and started out to Muddy Branch. On the way he pounced in the snow and chased along the deserted river bottom, yapping and tossing the flakes into the air. His hind feet made white cascades. He would bury his nose in the clean snow and then blow it into the sky with a flip of his head. For hours the fox danced around in the deepening snowflakes.

He ran out to the fields and looked across the farmlands. They were still and changed in this different world. Vulpes sat down by the fence and watched the cedar waxwings flying in clusters around the juniper trees searching for food in the winter morning. Their wistful, "Se-ee-ed, s-ee-d," carried across the lonely snow-filled hills. A group of energetic chickadees flitted along the fence row. They darted from limb to limb. Vulpes watched them swing upside down as they quickly scouted the underside of a twig for insects. All the while they called to each other in their scolding, "Chick-a-dee, chick-a-dee, chick-a-dee-dee-dee." A party of tufted titmice moved along with them. Their scolding notes blended with those of the chickadee. From the denser shrubby thickets came the musical tinks of the tree sparrows. Vulpes heard the pecking of the downy woodpecker and glanced toward the dead stub where the woodpecker was working. He saw a brown creeper drop from a high limb in a swooping flight to the base of a nearby tree. The creeper spiraled slowly up the trunk, searching the bark for insects. High in the tree tops flitted a loose flock of golden-crowned kinglets.

Vulpes set out to look for food. He walked into the field and looked at the bottom of every clump of grass where mice might be. Then he zig-zagged back and forth to search the small mounds in the snow. The mice were under the white blanket, working their way around the field looking for seeds and roots. As they went they made little puffy tunnels that branched out and threaded the field with avenues of snow mounds. When he caught a hot scent Vulpes would pounce on the end of these plowed hills and dig down into the snow to find his quarry.

The story of his search for mice was left behind him in the snow. With each adventure his trail marked what he had done. All across the field the tell-tale pattern lay in busy footsteps.

The snow was falling more slowly now. Except
for a few small flakes, it had almost stopped. Down
the river, below Muddy Branch, old Will Stacks, the
trapper, sat on the edge of his iron bed. He rubbed
his eyes and looked through the window of his
shack at the snow.

Will put on his long woolen underwear and pulled
on a pair of old warm trousers. After he had put on
his boots and tucked his pant legs down into them,
he built a fire in the old potbellied stove. While it
roared and crackled he made a pot of coffee.

Will Stacks was a lean man of about fifty. He

wasn't very tall, but was strong and wiry. He had a slight stoop and a bright shock of sandy-brown hair that was growing white around the temples. His face was tanned by the wind and sun until it had grown leathery and lined with deep wrinkles. Will Stacks lived alone in his little whitewashed shack on River Road. He trapped all fall and part of the winter, and all summer he fished on the breaks.

When Stacks had finished his cereal, he pulled on a sweater and opened the door to look at the weather. It was still snowing and the air was quite warm.

He went back to his oak table, sat down on a bench he had made one winter during idle hours, and sipped a hot drink. He thought about the traps that he would use today for foxes. Will trapped many animals: muskrats, mink, skunks and otter. This day, however, he would set them only for the red fox as he knew their furs were in their prime in December.

Will kept his traps in a slanting shed that opened off his one-room house. They hung from the wall or were kept in boxes according to size and type. There were some for foxes with big iron jaws; there were smaller ones for mink. Around the shed hung the tanned skins of many animals.

When Will had seen the snowstorm coming the day before, he had spent the afternoon checking his pack-basket and equipment to see that he had all the scents, lures and other things ready. Though it was more difficult to trap in the snow, from his long years of experience old Will Stacks knew just how to do it. The snow was perfect. It was fluffy and crisp, and the weather was not cold enough to crust the top or to freeze the spring of the trap.

Earlier in the year Will Stacks had mixed a brew that he had devised through the years, and had dropped his traps into it to remove the smell of steel. He made it by placing a big kettle on the stove and putting in it sassafras and maple bark, walnut hulls and various wood chips.

After he had done that, he spent one whole week brewing the lure, by a secret formula that his father had passed on to him. No one, not even his friend Buck Queen, knew how he made the scent which lured the fox off his trail and over to his trap. It was brewed from the musky glands of the muskrat to which fish oil and rancid butter were added. To this a few drops of skunk essence was added and an ounce or so of fox scent. Several drops of glycerine made it hold its odor in the rain and snow.

When it was completed, Stacks poured it in a little jar and kept it in the cool shed.

Will finished his cereal and put on his big mackinaw. He went into the shed and picked up his trapping basket, slung it over his lean shoulders and walked out into the snow.

The trapper had favorite locations for his fox traps. These he had found through years of trapping and hunts with Buck Queen during which the two men had studied the hills and glens the foxes roved.

He knew that the red fox liked the hills and abandoned fields where the grass was not too thick and heavy. He did not like the wet thicket regions where the gray fox moved, but kept to the open trails of other animals.

Sometimes he set his traps so far away that he had to take his car and drive four or five miles to the locations. Others were on the hillsides nearer home and he would walk to these in all weather. Will had about ten traps out already and this morning he was going to set three more. He planned to place them in and around Muddy Branch.

Crossing the field, he saw Vulpes' tracks in the snow. He studied them carefully to see where he had gone and what he had been doing. The zig-zagged trail told him that Vulpes had been hunting for mice under the snow. He also saw where he had followed a rabbit. If he had caught him, Stacks knew the fox would eat only what he needed and cache the remainder in a scooped-out pit in the earth. Later he would return and finish it.

Will imitated these store holes in his trappings. He went over to the fence row where Vulpes had slipped under the rail to the open field. Here he put down his pack and took out his trowel. He dug into the snow, being careful to stand in the same footsteps he made as he approached. Vulpes was crafty and Will Stacks knew it. He had to be clever to fool him. The snow was only a few inches deep by the fence, so he dug down into the earth just far enough to seat the trap firmly.

Then he made a small hole for the bait just above

the trap and put in a piece of rabbit. He drove a stake into the ground to which the open trap was chained. It sank into the bare ground, and Stacks placed the trap over it, setting it solidly in earth. He carefully wrapped up the dirt he had removed in a canvas cloth and put it in his pack. He knew he must not leave any dirt around or Vulpes would become suspicious.

Now, he replaced the snow around the jaws of the trap. He took great care not to let the snow slide under the trigger for if the trigger was jammed with snow or earth, the trap would not spring. With a little piece of paper as a guard he dropped the snow around the jaws. Then he filled up the hole until it looked as if a fox had dug it. He opened his bottle of scent and put a few drops of the potent lure over the traps. He had finished his work.

Old Will Stacks stood up and walked away. His trail through the snow looked as if he had not stopped to make the trap setting. He did it quickly so that his own scent would not linger around the spot.

Will looked up at the sky. By the blue-gray clouds he knew it would snow again before night. Perhaps it would be a light snow and the last scent of his trail would be covered. It would then be a perfect set.

He hurried down through the woods to Muddy Branch, walking surely and unhesitatingly to an open spring on the side of a hill. He had used this spot before and had caught many foxes here. He called this a water trap. He would place stepping stones in the spring which led to his lure as he knew the red fox did not like to get his feet wet. The fox would use these to approach the bait.

Old Will Stacks set his second trap, rose and disappeared through the woods.

Meanwhile, about half a mile away, Vulpes was

sleeping on a log on a hillside protected from the wind and snow. Vulpes had left the field where he had been searching for mice and had trotted off toward the woods in pursuit of game.

He had followed the trail of a rabbit into the woods, leaving the pattern in the snow that Will Stacks had seen.

As the rabbit scent grew warmer, Vulpes trailed his prey more cautiously. He was running easily now over the deep snow. Whenever he reached a vantage point as he closed in on his prey, he would stop and look over the woods. Here and there were clues left behind the hopping cottontail. He had girdled the young shoots of the shrubby hazelnuts. In places Vulpes could see where he had snipped the twigs in half. Beneath the wild roses and berry bushes the leaves were scattered over the snow. The rabbit had dug down to the ground to find any berries that might have fallen to the earth.

Then the trail would lead on. The big hind feet of the cottontail made long tracks in the white snow as he hopped along. They were punctuated with smaller tracks of his front feet.

On many occasions Vulpes had learned the speed that these long hind legs gave the rabbit. The rabbit was the only woodland creature who could match or better the speed of Vulpes. He knew that if he had to meet him in an open chase the rabbit would probably gain the safety of some burrow before he could catch him. But the fox knew he was more than a match in wits with the cottontail.

On a hillside the rabbit trail led off into a thicket of laurel. Here the footsteps were farther apart as the rabbit had sped from the swoop of a Cooper's hawk. Vulpes came closer. He could see where the hawk had actually landed in the snow and had followed him into the thicket with the relentless savage fury of an accipiter.

The fox looked closely to see if the hawk had got his prey. But the rabbit's trail wound through the gnarled shrub trunks to a little crevasse in some rocks where he had taken shelter. The warm scent still hung under the heavy canopy of leaves. There was a little scoop in the snowy leaves where the warm body of the cottontail had melted the flakes. When his enemy had flown off, the rabbit had come out of his hiding place and loped off again through the woods. Vulpes picked up his trail on the other side of the laurel thicket and followed him down the hill to the valley.

The rabbit seemed to be following an old game trail that led down the side of the hill. Vulpes began to calculate the manner in which he would outwit the speedy rabbit. He thought of the cottontail's big eyes set far back on either side of his head. With them he could detect any movement in almost any direction. Vulpes thought at times that he must be able to see behind him, he was so quick to jump. Then he decided what he would do. He would circle the trail the rabbit was following and lie in wait along it and take him by surprise as he came hopping along looking for food. He must do it quickly for the wind would be blowing his scent toward the rabbit if he got below him.

Vulpes sniffed the air. The rabbit was not far ahead. With a flash he skirted the crest of the hill and came down into the valley. He was below the rabbit. Cunningly he selected a spot for his ambush. It was off to the side of the old game trail where he could watch the path. A slight wind blew his tell-tale scent off to the side. A patch of snow-covered laurel leaves concealed his bright orange-red fur on the side where the rabbit would approach. He waited patiently.

Presently he saw the rabbit coming along the trail, his nose quivering in the air as he sought out the tender saplings.

Vulpes was ready. When the rabbit came in range he sprang. It was over. His chase was won.

Vulpes finished his meal and curled up on a log on the hillside. Under the snow not far from the log lay the food he had not eaten. With his slender black feet he had scraped away the frosted flakes of snow and had dropped it in the hole. He had covered it carefully with the snow using his nose as a shovel. When he was hungry he would come back for the rest of his meal. His cache looked very much like the trap set old Will Stacks had made along the edge of the field. But Vulpes did not know of the threat and slept easily for several hours.

Again in the late afternoon the leaden skies spilled their burden. First a fine splatter of chilled raindrops fell. A few snowflakes came with the rain. But with the cold of the gathering darkness, the rain turned to sleet and the snow grew thicker. Finally, hailstones formed high in the sky and lent their force of violence to the storm. The rain, sleet, snow and hail rasped through the countryside. The sound of their impact on the fallen snow droned through the fields and woods.

Old Will Stacks, the trapper, sat before the fireplace in his cabin. He listened to the rising fury of the storm as it beat against the roof above him. He walked to the curtainless window and looked out into the night. He scowled. This weather was not good. It would spoil his carefully made trap sets. Within a few hours, a thick crust of iced snow would cover the woodlands and settle over his traps. He had worked hard to make them spring with lightning swiftness. Now the icy crust would slow or even jam the action of his traps. He would have to reset them all in the morning and he didn't relish the task. He toyed with the idea of taking them in

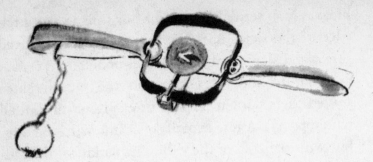

and ending the season. Already he had many prime pelts hanging in the cool shed that would bring good prices in the city. It had been a good season.

He went to his cupboard and took down some potatoes and beans to boil for supper.

"A poor set is worse than none at all," he mumbled as he pared the vegetables. "A bad set won't catch a thing. Merely scare the animal away and make him wise to my tricks. Guess I'll wait till morning and see if I should quit for the year."

Vulpes was roused from his slumbers by the storm. He raised his head and squinted into the night. The misty vapors of the bottoms were creeping up the floor of the valley. He heard the groaning creaks of heavy limbs sagging beneath the weight of the storm. Nothing was stirring in the woods. All the animals had sought shelter. The woodchucks and chipmunks were sleeping away the winter cold in their snug burrows deep in the earth. Bubo, the great horned owl, had sought his perch in a thick patch of evergreens. Vison, the mink, had slipped into his den along the creek. Procyon, the raccoon, stayed in his home in a hollow tree. In the bottoms, Urocyon, the gray fox, was curled in a hollow log.

Only Vulpes still lingered in the open. For a moment he thought of a den he had found in the rocks near-by. Then he dismissed the thought and tucked his nose beneath his warm bushy tail and pulled the bare pads of his feet close to his body. Now his thick tail covered the only exposed parts of his body—his nose and foot pads. For the moment he was quite comfortable and he went back to sleep. As the storm roared on, however, his log in the open became less pleasant. The wet sleet and rain dampened his coat. At times he found his fur freezing to the log. This annoyed him. He got up and trotted to the den in the rocks. He slipped beneath an overhanging rock that formed the entrance and curled up on the dry leaves and twigs. Soon his rhythmic breathing told he was asleep. Outside the storm blew on.

Toward morning the rain and sleet stopped. The rocks around Vulpes' den were glazed with ice. The footprints he had left in the snow as he took refuge the night before were silver pockets. As the early light hit the trees, their limbs burst into a cascade of shimmering lights. The whole woodland looked like a gigantic glass exhibit. Every blade of grass, every treetrunk was spun with ice. The streams in the valleys were Lucite ribbons. The hills sparkled and glistened.

Vulpes awoke and looked out of the dark den. He stepped out onto the ice gingerly. He had hardly gone three steps before his feet skidded on the slippery surface. He braced himself to keep from sliding. Then he made his way down the hazardous hill as fast as he could. When he reached the bottom he took the trail up the valley to the field where the land would not be so difficult.

As he came to the old rail fence Vulpes stood for a long time watching the sunlight strike over the glass hills. The white-throated sparrows called plaintively as they flitted over the weeds in the field. The seeds they needed for food were locked away from them by the ice. They flew from one field to another picking up food where they could. Sometimes they would find a bit in a corn stack under the bent leaves where it was protected from the sleet and ice. Haystacks offered occasional food. And in the shrubby fence rows, the thick, tangled bushes had sheltered a few scarce seeds from the weather.

Food was scarce. All the animals were moving over wide areas, hunting. The rabbits searched the ground. They found little to feed on. The quail were trying to scratch through the crust to reach the berries on the honeysuckle. Their small feet made little impression on the hard surface. Some of them had slept through the storm and were imprisoned beneath the ice.

As Vulpes watched the winter scene, he suddenly caught the musky scent of the lure old Will Stacks had put out. It came from the trail that wound through the fence near him. He went over to investigate. Stacks had used his winter lure, and in spite of the crust of ice a little of the strong odor came through.

Vulpes thought that some fox might have hidden a food supply. He scratched at the ice. As his claws finally broke through he caught the whiff of the bait that Will had planted. There was a sharp snap as the trap sprang!

Stacks was out of bed by this time. He was moving around in the cold morning, grumbling at the weather and trying to get the fire started.

About an hour later Stacks picked up his trapping basket and went out into the ice. He started his regular morning run of his trap line. The old trapper visited each set at least once a day.

He went over to the set he had made for Vulpes the day before. As he neared the trap he saw it had been sprung. But there was nothing in it.

A few black hairs from Vulpes' foot were caught in the closed jaws. With the spring of the trap Vulpes had jerked back. He felt the jaws slam shut as they grazed his forepaw. His backward leap sent him sprawling across the ice. Quickly, he regained his footing and vanished into the woods.

Thoroughly frightened, the fox sped dangerously fast across the treacherous ice to the wilderness of Muddy Branch.

Will Stacks looked at the sprung trap and knew what had happened. He also knew that he had made Vulpes a trap-wise fox.

"It'll be a long time before I fool that old fox again," he said, shaking his head. "Guess I'll bring my traps in for the season, except those few on the hill that are still all right."

Down in Muddy Branch Vulpes spent the next few days in the sanctuary of the isolated wilderness. Still unnerved by his experience with the trap, he did not even return to the hills above the Queen farm for many days.

In this weather, however, Vulpes was out almost any hour of the day or night. The ice had made it as difficult for him to find food as it had for the rabbits and quail. Some of the birds had even starved to death. To keep himself fed required all of Vulpes' time. He caught his prey when he could. He ate withered fruits. Some nights he went hungry.

Then one day the ice broke. A warm wind came in from the Southwest and the ice popped and peeled off the trees. The crust on the hill turned to slush and rolled down the valleys. Where the warm sun hit the sides of the hill, the snow melted and the leaves lay bare and soggy on the ground.

One evening as Vulpes lay curled on a stump in a little patch that lay free from the snow, he could

hear the leaves moving steadily a few feet away from him. He lifted his head and watched. He thought it might be a mouse, but his nose immediately caught the strong musky scent of Blarina, the short-tailed shrew.

Vulpes did not pounce upon him because he did not especially care for the shrew as food. Sometimes he was sorry for this for the woods were full of them. They tunneled and dug everywhere and were more numerous than mice.

Vulpes sat still and watched the long-snouted animal pry his way under the leaves in search of insects. Blarina was not pretty. He had small eyes almost hidden in his slick soft fur. He was lead brown in color and matched the decaying leaves of the floor of the woods where he crawled. He was short and dumpy. He was only about five inches long with a very short tail.

Blarina was so busy and so near-sighted that he didn't see Vulpes. But the fox could not be bothered with him. He had just finished his evening meal and pieces of it lay on the ground not three feet away from where he was resting.

Blarina caught the scent of the food. He ran over to it in a furious waddle, his nose twitching and turning. He leapt upon it savagely and tore it apart with a ferocity that surprised the fox. Hardly had he gulped down one piece before he darted to another and set upon it with the same rage. Vulpes thought Blarina had never eaten before, he ate so viciously. Then, the shrew caught the scent of Vulpes. As fast as his short legs would carry him he headed the other way and buried himself in the leaves.

A rising tunnel of loam marked his retreating trail as clearly as if he had been on top of the ground. Vulpes thought it was funny that Blarina would hide in this manner. For a long time he watched him burrow under the leaves and through the ground. But Blarina thought he was safe in the dark earth.

Presently the shrew hit one of the threads of an old run-way that he had made around the base of a hickory tree. It branched and turned, twisted and wove all over the woodland floor.

Now Vulpes could not tell where Blarina was. He could be in any one of the many complicated passages. He put his head down and went back to sleep.

December passed and January came. Vulpes was the handsomest fox in all of Maryland. His shrewdness had gained him respect and admiration in Muddy Branch.

One cold night when a light fresh snow lay pale blue in the moonlight, Vulpes wandered down to a partly frozen stream. Here he stopped and sniffed the air. He caught the musky smell of Vison, the mink, who was out hunting. He listened and heard Procyon, the raccoon, fishing down the creek. The tinkle of forming ice rang out through the quiet valley. Overhead he heard the soft muffled flight of Bubo, the great horned owl.

Vulpes was restless tonight. He trotted along the stream that threaded through the valley. He followed a trail over the hill above the Queen farm. As he passed he turned to look down on Brownie, the old Red Bone, and for a moment he thought he would call to him. But Vulpes did not want a chase. There was something new awakening within him that kept him racing over the Potomac River side.

Even Muddy Branch did not satisfy the fox. The fields where he loved to hunt mice seemed barren and ordinary. Vulpes ran far and free over the farmlands and woods in search of a mate.

CHAPTER SIX

As January passed and the hours of daylight grew longer, Vulpes left Muddy Branch for days at a time to wander toward the Blue Ridge Mountains.

One evening when the air was nippy and cold, Vulpes was drinking at a spring on the side of a mountain. The bubbling water spilled over the rocks and twisted through the woods. The fox crouched low to watch it as it came out of the side of the hill. It burst free from the earth with force and sang softly as it fell over the roots of a tree and ran through the glade.

While he listened to these new sounds near the spring, Vulpes heard footsteps behind him. They were the light footsteps of a fox. He looked up to see a lovely vixen coming toward him, carefully stepping on the rocks to keep her feet dry. The wind turned back the fur on Vulpes' back as he stood and watched her gliding toward him. She was young and strong. He twitched his tail and ran toward her leaping high over the spilling water.

The vixen checked her advance, turned, ran off into the woods several yards and looked back to see if Vulpes were following. He had circled her and was standing in the trail below, one foot resting on a log. Vulpes watched her closely.

They sprinted off through the woods, taking the trails she knew so well. As they traveled along the

mountain paths, her flirtations began to annoy Vulpes. She darted and dashed around his feet and scampered playfully into the leaves beside him.

As they chased each other about the forest, Vulpes would catch the scent of prey. The vixen, to show her talents, stalked in the direction that he had pointed. But she was nervous and excited and usually gave the game fair warning that she was approaching. A quail flew up before her, and a rabbit darted off when she rustled the dry leaves. Vulpes was dismayed by her carelessness.

By dawn, he knew this was not his mate. She would not follow him beyond the farms at the foot of Sugar Loaf Mountain, and hesitated when he dashed brazenly across an open field within view of a house. Her spirit of play and adventure left her. She became cowed and fearful when she wandered away from her native mountain trails. Vulpes could not help wondering how she would fare before Brownie and Joe in Muddy Branch. He felt she would not love the chase and the hunt. Then, he knew he wanted to return to Muddy Branch where every day was a new adventure and the hills resounded with the voice of Brownie and the call of Buck Queen. He was unhappy in the quiet woods of the mountain. The trails were unfamiliar and he missed the roar of the river. There was fine hunting here, but this was not his land.

At dawn Vulpes led the vixen to the foot of the hill and started out across the fields. She ran with him as far as a dirt road and then circled, barking and calling to him to run back with her to the mountains. Vulpes slid through the wire fence and stopped on the other side. She did not follow. He turned and started down the road. The vixen trotted along the inside of the fence, but Vulpes did not look back. She halted and watched him glide down the road. He disappeared into a small woodlot. She could not follow. His route lay through farms and fields and she needed the protective shadow of the old mountain. The vixen turned slowly and went back into the forest. In the distance she could hear the caw of crows as they followed Vulpes along the fence rows, through woodlots and down the lonely wagon roads.

Late that evening Vulpes came back to the River at Seneca, about five miles above Muddy Branch, after sleeping away the day in a farmland woods. He followed the small, deep stream to the canal locks at the river. As he came to the summer cottages along the creek, he left the water's edge and moved back to an old road. It ran along the bottom of a small knoll and was covered with leaves. Bushes hung over it, and thick mats of honeysuckle almost squeezed it out of sight. The road led to an old red sandstone sawmill that stood like a giant shell among the trees. Great tulip poplars grew up through its roof that had long since fallen in and rotted away. Years ago it had been a mill where quarried sandstones were sawed into building blocks. Rusty pieces of machinery lay on its sandy floor and the old mill race still passed the shaft where the waterwheel had been. Old worn automobile tires were scattered in the race and vines wound over the building. The mill looked desolate and dead in the grove of tall trees.

As Vulpes approached the mill, he saw a fox coming up the road. It was a vixen. The land was familiar to her and she passed the fallen walls of the old mill as easily as Vulpes passed the kennels of the Queen farm. He dashed toward her, barking in a low squall. Here was a vixen that knew the river bottoms and his homeland.

When she saw Vulpes she snarled in an acid voice. The fox stopped. He felt the challenge of the fierce female. Her daring spirit encouraged him and he came nearer. From the hillside of brush and tangled vines a dog-fox appeared. He slunk past the abandoned building and stood beside the female. His teeth were bared and his great brush twitched excitedly from side to side.

Vulpes understood that these two were mates, but he stood his ground. He was pleased by the big vixen's strength and boldness even though her warning growls were now long and deep.

Her dog-fox circled him. Vulpes kept his big brushy tail between himself and his opponent. Both foxes bared their fangs and watched each other over their shoulders as they stood side by side. The fur rose on their backs. Occasionally Vulpes jumped back as the tail of his opponent licked before his eyes. He felt no fear, for he knew he was larger and faster than his rival, but he was not sure he wanted to fight it out. This pair were mates, and his desire for the vixen was not strong enough to warrant a kill. However, he did flash his tail and leap toward the rival fox with enough ferocity to let him know he was master of the fight. Then Vulpes withdrew. The female did not snarl now as he passed her and moved down the road. She watched him walk slowly away. She turned to her mate and raced with him up the hillside and into the night woods. In a clearing, she looked back once more at the handsome fox, who was now standing in the road looking toward the frozen river.

Vulpes went down to the shore and listened with great satisfaction to the water breaking through the ice at the dam. Its dull roar soothed his restless spirit and he followed the great broad body of water toward Muddy Branch. He was glad to be again in the land where Brownie hunted and old Buck Queen admired his cunning.

At the dam he changed his direction and walked out along the jutting wall. In the misty distance below the waterfall he could see the islands that filled the river with their dark scattered shapes. Vulpes had never been to these islands, and now that the ice had bridged them with the main land he was tempted to visit these rich acres that smelt of grapes and fruit in the fall and of flowers and birds in the summer.

Cautiously, he stepped onto the rough ice that had jammed in great chunks below the dam and between the islands. Vulpes ran swiftly so that his weight would not break the thinner patches of ice and drop him into the cold swirling water. He darted for a big boulder that was jutting just above the frozen surface. Here he rested and judged what course he would take over the wide perilous stretch that lay before him. He calculated a circuitous route that led from one small island to the next. Below these small bodies of land, the water flowed in slow eddies, and had frozen solid in the zero weather.

Vulpes moved swiftly to the first island. He skirted the grasses and weeds for food, then leapt to the next. The dark outline of Grape Vine Island lured him on. The scent of sleeping quail and of rabbits came to him from the island as the wind drifted his way.

The last narrow stretch from a large boulder to Grape Vine Island was dangerous. Between the two a deep current rushed. The ice had formed thinly over the swift water and was barely strong enough for Vulpes' weight. He gathered his feet under him and made a swift dart. As he streaked across the barrier his feet touched the ice lightly, sending out white stars wherever they pressed. The stars moaned as they formed, shooting out to reach the shore just before Vulpes. The fox leapt to the sandy bank and glided up to a knoll to look across the island. It was rimmed with ancient elms that were bound together with drooping grape vines. The center of the island was cleared of all trees. It had once been a field where a farmer had planted crops and grazed cattle. Now it was overgrown with bushes and a few young saplings. Driftwood hung in the branches of the trees that surrounded it, marking the highwater level of a bygone flood. The fox stepped out into the field and sniffed the air. The scent of rabbits and mice smelt warm and heavy on the cold wind. Here was a rich hunting ground locked off from prowlers by the rough body of water.

Vulpes immediately hunted food and then settled down on the dry leaves under the elms to sleep away the rest of the night. Just before sunrise, when the sky was pale with light, he was awakened by the snap of a twig among the trees at the lower end of the island. He lifted his head.

In the shadows of the thin morning light he saw Fulva, the vixen red fox who lived alone on the island. She was the most beautiful fox Vulpes had ever seen. He rose slowly and looked at her intently.

She did not move a muscle, but stood with her head raised, at the foot of a tremendous elm whose roots were scooped bare by the flood waters. Her red-orange fur gleamed in the cool light.

Vulpes walked toward her, his tail stretched proudly behind him. When he was only a few feet from her he stopped. Fulva took one step toward him—and by that gracious movement Vulpes knew he had found his mate. There was no flirtatiousness in her like the vixen of Mount Sugar Loaf, nor did she have the fierceness of the Seneca vixen. Vulpes felt content before this gentle fox. His restless urge to roam the hills and fields subsided.

Vulpes went to her side and the two foxes walked quietly off through the spreading elms.

For several days they played and romped in the abandoned field. Vulpes found his mate a close match for him when he hunted mice and rabbits. She was not as swift, but she planned her attacks more carefully and she never missed. Fulva took him all over the big island. Sometimes at dusk they would cross to isles just beyond their own to hunt while the misty winter sun disappeared over the Virginia hills.

Fulva had been born on this island two years ago. During the summer her brothers and sisters had swum to the mainland, and with the great freeze of the next winter, her parents had followed. Fulva had remained behind. She liked the lonely island surrounded by water, the hunting, and the summers when the elms were green and singing with birds. The island belonged to her and she would awake in the evening, stretch and look quietly across her dark domain.

One night when the wind was blowing from the Maryland shore, it brought across the water the far, faint cry of Brownie. Vulpes pricked up his ears and listened. Through the lonely night the voice of the Red Bone brought back to him the thrill of the hunt, and Vulpes knew he must return to the rolling valleys and rocky hills. He looked at the sleeping Fulva and lifted his head into the wind. He would take her back to his land where the bluebells opened in the spring and the kinglets filled the treetops with their sweet pensive calls, and where the miles rolled under the feet of the fox who led the chase.

Fulva awoke as if called and saw her mate trembling as he breathed the shore blown wind. He went down to the water's edge and looked out into the dark night. Vulpes looked back at Fulva. She had followed him to the sandy bank, lifting her head and sniffing the air to find on the wind a scent of the disturbance that had awakened her mate.

Then Vulpes crossed the thin ice to the rock beyond the channel. She knew he wanted her to follow. Vulpes had been awakened by the call of the great Maryland shore lands and was ready to return to his home. She hesitated for a moment; then darted across the ice to the rock where he stood.

Vulpes nudged her and would have loitered on the rocks near her home, but Fulva had made her decision. She dashed off the rock onto the jammed ice and ran toward the distant shore. However, Vulpes led the way from island to island, changing his old route where the ice had turned to water, and finding new jams of snow and rocks.

When they came to the Maryland shore, Vulpes dashed up the bank to the tow-path. Fulva followed swiftly. Together they ran through the woods, crossed the canal on the ice and sprinted down the dark valleys to the beautiful stream that drifted under the ancient beeches and broad oaks.

Fulva never thought of her island again, for Vulpes filled their nights and days with exciting explorations and she never tired of following her mate's trails over the land. Some led to the open farms beyond River Road where cattle grazed and lights from the houses gleamed like yellow eyes in the night. Some penetrated deep into the thickets where rabbits nested. And one led overland to the hill above the Queen farm.

As Fulva followed her mate up this hill to its high top, she caught the smell of hounds and men. She was instinctively afraid but Vulpes led her on until they stood on the highest crest and looked down on the kennels and chicken coops below. A curl of gray smoke rose from the chimney of the house and one light gleamed in the kitchen window where Buck Queen was still moving about.

While Fulva looked down on the scene with mixed temerity and awe, Vulpes put his head down and called to Brownie. She heard the rattle of chains as the Red Bone came out of his kennel and walked to the end of the chain's length. Brownie was glad to hear the voice of the red fox and answered with a

long howl. Fulva could hear him tug at the chain that held him fast.

The vixen retreated down the trail and watched her mate from the green safety of a laurel bush. The strange tie between the hound and the fox was new to her. She did not understand this friendship.

After several weeks of roaming the hills, Fulva had less and less desire to follow her mate on his playful and far flung explorations. She preferred to stay on a sheltered hillside that stood like a bluff over Muddy Branch. Some new feeling had come over her and she sought the sun on the south side of the hill. It was a pleasant feeling of peace like the first spring thaw when the earth is mellow with the anticipation of spring.

One night Vulpes returned from a hunt to find her digging beneath the roots of an old beech tree on the knoll. She had tunneled in several feet and her fur was dusty with earth. When she heard him approach she came out and shook the dirt from her back. Vulpes understood that she wanted a den.

They stopped only to sleep and hunt in the fields, but Fulva slept lightly and hunted without much interest. She was always anxious to return to the beech tree and dig away the dry clay that lay beneath the dark loam of the woodland floor.

By the middle of March they had finished their home.

It sloped into the ground from the foot of the tree for about fifteen feet. Two entrances led off the main tunnel at the end of which was a small hollow a little more than a foot across. The den was neat and clean, lined only with the sandy clay of the earth. Fulva had carefully scattered the freshly dug earth down the bluff so that the entrance would be inconspicuous. The leaves blew over it until the foxes' den blended into the woodland floor.

CHAPTER SEVEN

In late March Vulpes noticed a change in Fulva's attitude toward him. She did not want to be with him any more. She no longer went hunting with him or romped and played along the woodland trails. When he would call to her to follow him over the rocks to the canal, she turned her back and crawled deep into their den.

She stayed in the earth a greater part of the night and day and only came out to hunt when a mouse ran near the den. One night Vulpes came bounding over the knoll to bring her out for a trip to the fields where the quail were roosting. Fulva snarled as he entered the den. He came in a little farther to be sure he had heard correctly. Fulva bared her teeth and growled long and loud. Her hostility was very clear and Vulpes withdrew. He did not understand why, but he knew Fulva wanted to be alone.

Hurt and disappointed, he walked out to the field to search for the quail. That night he returned to the den many times to see if Fulva would join him. She would not. Once he brought a mouse as a present. He dropped it at the entrance of the den by the roots of the big beech tree. As he lay on his haunches before the earth, looking curiously into the dark, he heard Fulva coming down the long tunnel. He pricked up his ears and ran joyfully toward her, but she did not respond. Fulva took the food quickly and returned to the dark interior. Vulpes cocked his head to one side and watched her with wonder as she went back, snarling softly.

He slept in the leaves near the den that day and at evening wandered alone to the hill above the Queen farm. Later that night he returned to the beech tree with more food. This time Fulva did not come out. He waited long for her to appear, and when she did not, he walked off into the cool woodlands by himself.

The following night he came back with a rabbit and laid it gently beside the untouched mouse. No sooner had he put it down than Fulva flashed out and pounced on it hungrily. She retreated to the earth, giving Vulpes no encouragement to follow.

Vulpes went down to the stream and sat on a log.

He brushed his fur with his tongue and shined the soft white patch on his breast. He knew that the beautiful mate he had so carefully selected no longer needed him. On the other side of the stream he could still see their footprints in the snow on the northern exposure. They were rapidly disappearing as the warm air circled into the valley from the high sun-lit hills. They were in a single line and led like the trail of one into the trees. He remembered how they had so often traveled, one behind the other, using the same footprints so that only the eagle eye of one as familiar with the fox as Will Stacks or Buck Queen would recognize the trail of two.

Vulpes sat alone on the log until dawn. As if by some unseen signal the white-throated sparrows filled the woods around him with their flute-like melodies. He looked up to see the yellow-green buds of the spice bush opening to the sun. Along the slope of the creek the sepals of the trailing arbutus had folded back to let the fragrant pink blossoms uncurl. Overhead a red-shouldered hawk sped through the air in loops and spirals and dived, screaming, through the lacy tops of the bursting willow trees.

It was spring again. The dark earth was warm and moist. Pockets of water had collected in the woodland hollows and trickled in small rivulets to the stream below. A party of bluebirds paused along the water's edge, their soft mellow "churls" floating down through the woods on the humid winds of spring. A cardinal sat like a red berry on the hickory tree above the fox.

A change had come to the woodlands and Vulpes was part of this new life. On the bluff above the stream Fulva lay with his newborn pups.

The next week Vulpes spent almost all of his waking hours hunting for both Fulva and himself. Her appetite was tremendous and he had difficulty keeping her fed.

One morning when the air was warm and sweet, and the woods were full of the songs of the birds, Fulva came out of the den. She blinked in the bright light and shook the dust from her fur. Vulpes walked up to her cautiously. She jumped into the air and chased him for a few steps, then ran down to the creek and lapped the cold water. From the stream bed she barked at Vulpes, calling him down to the water's edge. Vulpes came gliding down, still a little hesitant for fear she would turn on him again. But she did not. She seemed willing and glad to play. However, she would not leave the site of the den, and occasionally stopped to look back at it. Vulpes would look back too; the den was quiet and almost hidden by flowers and pale green leaves. Above it, the mellow carol of a thrush made the den seem magical to the fox.

After an hour or so of frolicking, Fulva went back to the den and stretched out beside the beech tree to rest. Vulpes stood his distance, momentarily expecting her to growl and disappear. For a long time he watched the door of the den with anticipation and then walked off a few yards. He heard a small weak whimper. Vulpes stepped carefully toward his earth.

In the dark entrance he could see two small eyes shining, and then a round fuzzy pup rolled out into the spring sun. The old fox sat down on his

haunches and looked. A second pup followed this one out into the light and wobbled over to Fulva.

The pups stretched their fat legs and sat uncertainly on a big green leaf of a young May-apple. A few minutes later two more pups came out. They stood timidly at the door of the den and looked across the bright woodlands to the flowing stream. Another one followed them. The fox cocked his head and looked down the tunnel to see if there were more. A sixth pup came running past the roots and scampered into the leaves barking and biting his brothers and sisters. The six little foxes played with their mother and barked at Vulpes when he came near. He wanted to play with them and teach them to hunt immediately, but Fulva guarded them jealously.

While he was watching her brush their gray fur with her tongue, another little fox came out of the dark den and circled around her mother. Vulpes went over and peered down the tunnel just as an eighth pup rolled past him, and, frightened by his father's presence, scurried under the white fur of his mother's breast.

Vulpes went over to the highest point of the knoll and curled up proudly on a rock. He couldn't go to sleep although he closed his eyes as if he were not impressed with his big family. He kept opening

one eye, however, to watch his eight little foxes
kicking up the leaves and chasing flies in the sunlight. Suddenly his attention was attracted to the
den again, and Vulpes looked over to see a robust
pup, the ninth, walk out into the air, sniffing and
looking nonchalantly around. The ruddy little cub
glanced at his brothers and sisters and then walked
right over to Vulpes. The fox got up and peered at
him curiously, as the audacious pup clambered up
the slope and sat down before him. Vulpes sniffed
him and touched his soft fur with his nose. For a

moment he did not know what to do and looked to Fulva. She was stretched out with the eight pups suckling her, and all happy and content in the sun. Suddenly Vulpes felt a surge of strength go through him—all these helpless little animals were his and they were depending on him for food and protection. He gently shoved the audacious pup back to Fulva and set out proudly to hunt food. At the crest of the next hill he turned to look back. The slope was bouncing with puppies. Nine of them.

Vulpes walked with his head high in the air until he was out of sight and then burst into a run. Swiftly he headed for the field where the mice and rabbits were abundant. In a few hours he was back with food for Fulva. She had taken the pups inside and was waiting for Vulpes at the den.

Strange noises and scents alarmed Fulva for the next few weeks. She would dash from the den at the sound of Bubo or the snap of a stick. One evening she scanned the countryside carefully and then went back into the den and led out the audacious pup. Vulpes watched her take him off into the woods for a short distance. She led him to an open space where Blarina, the shrew, was tunneling under the loam. The pup looked up at his mother and then down at the moving mound. For a moment he stood uncertainly, then with a sudden spurt he leapt upon the ground and scratched vigorously. Blarina had felt the disturbance and slipped off through the underground avenue. But the audacious pup dug on. After he had broken through to the tunnel he sniffed the ground and ran back to his mother. Fulva took him back to the den. As he went he hopped on every stirring leaf and flower.

Vulpes had noticed a further change in Fulva since the pups were born. She was fierce and bold. She had lost much of her tenderness and warmth and was alert to every danger. Only when she was with the pups, nursing them or smoothing their rumpled coats, was she the gentle mate he had known.

The burden of the hunting was put on Vulpes for Fulva guarded her offspring with a constant and untiring vigil.

One morning when Vulpes was out looking for food, he came to the field that bordered the woods of Muddy Branch near River Road. A large farm stretched out beyond. Cattle were grazing the short green grasses. As he crouched in the fence row, half hidden by the leaves and vines, Vulpes saw two men coming across the field. He was alarmed and flashed back to the bluff to warn Fulva.

The men Vulpes had seen were Charlie Craggett and Cy Cummings, two farmers who owned the fields that joined the woods. Charlie was an aged man with gray hair and brown eyes. He was an expert farmer and worked hard to make his land produce. His neighbor, Cy Cummings owned about twenty-nine head of cattle that he had raised and bought over the many years he had lived along the Potomac River bottom. Both men were friends of Buck Queen and often went on hunts with him in the fall and winter when the sport of the hunt lured them all from their fields.

Cy had lost a young heifer early that morning and he had called on Charlie to help him find her and bring her in. They were walking down through the field that was growing green with the thin blades of winter wheat.

"I didn't mend that hole in the edge of the fence near Muddy Branch last year, and I suspect she got out that way," Cy was saying when Vulpes saw him.

"Well, she can't get far," Charlie said, slinging the rope he was carrying over his shoulders and striding carefully down the plowed wheat fields.

Both men were glad to be out in the spring air, and the smell of fresh wet loam was good to them. At the fence, the hoof prints of the heifer were cut deeply in the springy topsoil.

"Yes, she headed for the woods and the flowers,"

Cy laughed as he followed the young cow's trail. It crossed the ridge and went down into the valley and out across the flats carved by the stream. There among the fresh bushes was the heifer, browsing on the new leaves. The two men had little trouble catching her and were turning to lead her back when Charlie stooped below the limbs of the young saplings and peered across the stream.

"I'll bet that little hole under that beech tree is a fox den," the keen-eyed farmer said as he pointed to the bluff.

"It's about the right size and shape," Cy said as he located the position Charlie had pointed out to him. "Say, I believe they have pups at this time of year. Want to go over and take a look? I'll tie the heifer here."

"Sure, I've never seen a fox cub," Charlie answered. "Let's see if we can get one out." Cy tied the rope that was looped around the heifer's neck to a tulip poplar tree and the two men went down to the water's edge to look for a crossing. They found a tree foot-log that had fallen across the creek and ran across it balancing themselves with their arms. On the other side they leapt to the ground and trotted purposefully up the hill to the bluff.

Fulva heard them coming and sped deep into the den with the nine pups. She crouched back against the earth and watched the tunnel, trembling and frightened, her strong muscles drawn up like wires.

Charlie rested when he reached the top of the steep climb and waited for Cy. The men walked over to the opening and bent down to look in.

"This has just been used recently," Charlie said picking up the loose earth.

"Sure, there is probably a litter in there right now," added Cy. "Look at the rabbit and mouse bones around here in the leaves."

Charlie put his arm down the tunnel and reached as far as he could. The roots of the big tree stuck his shoulder and he could feel nothing.

"That sure goes way back," he said. "I wish we had a shovel and could dig them out."

"It's right hard to dig out a used den," Cy said, shaking his head. "A fox makes pretty sure that it winds its tunnel around a lot of roots and rocks— and they go awfully deep."

The men tried a few more times to reach into the den, but to no avail. Cy stood up and shook the dust off his arm.

"Well, I guess we won't see a pup today. We'd better get the heifer and go on back," he said as he turned and started down the bluff. The men crossed the stream along the log, untied the heifer and led the reluctant animal back through the woods and home.

Fulva heard them go. Vulpes darted from a hiding place near the den and slipped out onto the bluff as the men walked off through the woods. He went back to the den and smelt the fresh odor of their hands on the earth. Deep in the den he heard his pups whimpering. Fulva was still with them, her head pressed against the roof of the hollow. She knew what she must do, and waited until all sounds and smells of the men had left the area.

She picked up a pup in her mouth and walked down the tunnel and out into the air. Without stopping she went back over the hill and down the other side. She traveled across several hills with her burden, and put him gently down in a rocky cave where Vulpes had hidden from the storm last winter. The little pup curled up in the leaves in the shelter and went to sleep. Fulva returned for another one.

Pup by pup, she moved her family to the new site. The men had found their home. She did not know when they might return. If they did, they would not find a trace of a fox.

Late that night Fulva had all nine of her cubs in the dry leaves of the rock cave. Here they were not protected as well as they had been in the deep den.

She knew her job to protect the unschooled and helpless youngsters against the wild dangers of the woods would be much more difficult now.

Vulpes sensed Fulva's problems and stayed near the rock cave, hunting the valleys nearby for food. One night while out scouting, he caught the scent of Vison, the mink. He was coming down to the edge of the small streamlet that ran below the cave. Vulpes heard his pups romping in the moonlight. They were big enough now to come down the hill to the valley below to play and explore.

The fox sensed the danger of the situation and decided to head off Vison. He stole down to the stream several yards away from the mink and splashed lightly in the water. Vison heard the water break. He looked up. It sounded as if a frog had jumped into a pool. Sliding along the edge of the stream, he moved stealthily toward the disturbance. Vulpes moved silently toward him. He growled softly. Vison lifted his head and listened. He slipped into the creek and swam to the other side. The mink disappeared in the night. Vulpes watched him go. He knew there was no fear in this powerful animal who moved like a flash of light and could easily slash to pieces enemies larger than himself.

But Vison was in no mood to take on the swift Vulpes and he left the stream for the deep woods.

That night Vulpes brought home a mouse and hid it in the leaves and twigs by the cave. The pups were exposed to dangers in their new home and must learn to hunt as early as possible. When they smelt the buried mouse they stalked it carefully. Then they would arch into the air and drop upon it in one swift motion. As their paws came down, their teeth struck through the leaves to the buried mouse.

Fulva took care of most of the training, but Vulpes often went out into the woods with the audacious pup who was learning more rapidly than the others. He taught him where to find grasshoppers and fruits, and showed him the trails that the rabbits took to the fields. The audacious pup was full of spirit and eager to follow his father on all his travels.

One evening while they were walking along the road side, the audacious pup carefully placing his paws in his father's footsteps, Vulpes stopped and sniffed the air. The pup stopped and lifted his nose, too. Buck Queen was returning home with two dogs. Vulpes shoved the cub into a hollow log and brushed him down with his tail. The little fellow felt the fear of the impending crisis and crouched quietly in the shelter.

His father went off to a hill and watched the old

hunter come down the road. He kept a line of trees between himself and the man. Buck was not hunting, and one of the dogs was on a leash. The other was heeling. Buck had taken the two setters out to a nearby field to train them in the art of hunting quail. Freckles, the pup, was on the leash. He was exhausted by the afternoon of training and walked homeward obediently. Dash, the older dog, was thoroughly trained and had fallen behind Buck on the order, "Heel." Here he pranced eagerly as though restrained by an invisible chain, hoping for a word from his master that would send him flying through the thickets searching for game. But Buck was on his way home and the order did not come.

Vulpes relaxed as they passed, but did not take his eyes away from the trio. When they had rounded the bend, he turned to bring out his pup again, but the little fox was already standing beside him.

His forehead was wrinkled and he was watching these new animals with tremendous interest. Vulpes knew it would not be long before he must take the little fellow to the hill above the Queen farm and teach him about man.

CHAPTER EIGHT

The heat of summer rode in with June. The river trickled over the dam and the great gneiss and sandstone boulders that obstructed its course lay dry and bare in the water. In the cave, Vulpes and Fulva and the nine cubs were buried from sight by a heavy growth of summer grasses and leaves. Occasionally in the depths of night when the dew was on the grass, Fulva would take a cub out to the fields to hunt mice.

Late one night when she was out with the audacious pup she jumped high over the grasses to show him how to leap clear of the long blades and scan the field for movement. The cub liked these excursions and would leap in the air proudly. Then he saw his Mother rise on her hind feet and stand there as she looked over the grasses. This delighted the youngster and he tried to imitate her. But no sooner would he push himself up than he came tumbling down again. He worked at this trick until dawn lighted the eastern sky and it was time to go home.

The audacious pup was disappointed that his adventures were over and followed her reluctantly to the end of the field. At the woods he tried once more to rise to his hind feet. Suddenly, he found himself balanced comfortably and surveying the area with his dark paws dangling in front of him. He looked over the field and sniffed the air. Then he caught a jerky movement at the far end of the lot. His ears shot forward in anticipation. As he watched he realized that the movement was strange to him although not unfamiliar. Somewhere in his memory he connected it with Buck Queen. Hot pangs of fear shot through him. It was a man—Will Stacks, who was out to fish the river for catfish. It was early in the year, but he was already beginning to gather the ingredients for his fox lure that he would mix in the fall for another year of trapping. Will was now after fish oil. He crossed the field at the river end and went out to untie his rowboat and pole to the deep holes.

The audacious pup had seen enough. Forgetting his accomplishment he darted past his mother and hurried over the hills to the cave.

That night Vulpes was standing in the midst of his nine large pups, trying to hold his own against flying paws and whisking tails when he heard the call of Bubo, the great horned owl.

The fox did not move. Perhaps this was the chance he had waited for for so long: for Bubo to dive at his cubs. If he did, Vulpes would reward himself with a mouthful of feathers or the old owl himself. He waited like a set trap.

Above, in a hickory tree, Bubo was looking the situation over carefully. He saw the sly red fox and thought better of whatever he had in mind. He was

not hungry anyhow, and the cubs were rather large to trifle with. Furthermore, his own family of this new spring, had flown from the nest and were hunting on their own. As he saw no chance for a successful attack, he decided he preferred mice and flew silently off through the trees. Vulpes licked his jaws as he watched the owl float like a shadow over the hills. He looked down at his family.

Fulva had returned from the stream where she was schooling a young vixen. They had caught several frogs in the boggy leaves and were bouncing up the hill, well fed, to join the family. Several pups frolicked off to meet them and all came back to the cave, yapping in chorus. Fulva sensed the alarm in Vulpes. She knew it was either Bubo or Vison, for she was aware of her mate's particular distaste for the old owl and the strong mink. Their communications were limited and she could only guess the reason for his tenseness.

As the summer wore on, Vulpes became less attentive to his cubs. They were hunting for themselves now and doing well in the valley of Muddy Branch. Occasionally he would go off with one of them on a rabbit chase, but that had almost stopped now. He spent a large part of his time on the hill above the Queen farm. Several times he raced with Brownie and Joe through the hills and fields. Buck was getting them in trim for the coming hunting season and it was not unusual for Vulpes to waken in the morning with the sound of Brownie's voice ringing through the leafy woods. Off the two would go, recapturing the spirit of the autumn when both hound and fox thrilled to the chase.

In early September it began to rain. It rained steadily and long. A tropical hurricane was moving up the coast and all along its margins the rains were falling heavily. The skies were leaden for many days. The pups, now ruddy and handsome, sought shelter in the cave and confined their explorations to the hills near-by.

One night when the rain was pelting the hills and digging little holes in the road that circled Buck Queen's place, Vulpes went down to the river. The bare rocks were covered and the dam was buried under a sheet of water. The lacy rush of the falls had changed. It was dull and heavy-sounding. The whole river groaned and moved swiftly along its bed. While Vulpes was watching the great muddy body moving over the land, the water reached up and lapped around his feet. The gnarled willows along the bottom were standing in the swirling river. There was no sharp cut to mark the line where the river ended and the land began. These trees spent much of the early months of the year with their roots in the water, and clusters of dried leaves and boards high in their limbs marked the water level of previous floods. They hung like old birds' nests from almost every limb.

Vulpes was not alarmed by the rising water and returned home along the canal, leisurely hunting berries. When he reached the mouth of Muddy Branch, he noticed that these placid waters were swollen and swift. The land was different and the stream smelled strongly of decayed leaves and fish. The fox hurried up the hill to the cave. A few cubs were nearby, but many of them were out hunting in the rain. Fulva was not around. He curled up in a

laurel thicket to shield himself from the weather.

He woke often during the night to hear the powerful groaning of the river as it moved over the land. The sound of its fury came closer and closer. Vulpes got up several times and anxiously looked for his family. Once or twice he trotted down to Muddy Branch and was now alarmed to find the stream had burst its banks and was running wild across the valley.

Procyon, the raccoon, climbed a sycamore tree to his den far above the water. Moles that lived along the water's edge were fleeing before the growing wrath of the river. They were frightened and uncomfortable without a nest or burrow to dive in when the prowlers of the night threatened them.

A squirrel raced from limb to limb, uncertain and confused in the dark. He had gone to sleep in a tree along the edge of the river at dusk and was frightened from his rest when the waters, digging the earth from beneath the roots of the yellow poplar in which he slept, had tipped it into the current.

Vulpes went back to the cave and waited for his cubs to return. The rain was still pouring out of the sky. Toward morning five of the pups returned and wandered restlessly around the rocky hill. The fox thought he should lead them to higher ground, but his concern for Fulva and the other youngsters kept him close to the cave.

By dawn the water was creeping over the bottom-lands and in many cases had linked the canal and the river.

Old Buck Queen got up early. He walked down through the woods to see how high the river had come during the night. He was uneasy about his kennels and chicken coops, but was more concerned about the little old lady who lived in a house by herself on the edge of the canal. She had opened and closed the locks years ago when barges of coal and grain moved along the inland waterway. Several times before she had had to move before the rising river, and though she knew it would happen again and again, she always returned to her old home. Buck thought he would have to help her. The rain had not let up and the water was still rising. Hardly had he left his farm when he met the river. It lapped gently at the fence posts that marked off Mrs. Violet's yard. Buck rolled his boots up to his hips and waded through the water that was now nearly a foot deep on the old lady's lawn.

Mrs. Violet, however, had listened to the river all night and knew that she must leave again. She had packed her most cherished belongings, carried a few

chairs and dishes to the second floor and was standing on her front porch shaking her fist at the water, telling it to go back.

"It's a mean river," she called to Buck when she felt his footsteps on the porch. The little old lady was almost eighty-six and her eyesight had gone back on her.

"It's going to be a bad one this time," Buck said as he picked up her bag. "Can I take some more things upstairs for you?"

"No, one of the boys is coming down from the farm on the hill," she said, clutching her cane and feeling for the edge of the porch. "Just get me out of here. I'm good and mad at that river."

Will Stacks was up early also. He was out in his shed gathering together his traps and trapping equipment and storing them in his car. He had taken the covers off his iron bed and had thrown the mattress across the beams of the shed. The water was to his door, and he had brought his rowboat up from the river and chained it to the back porch, where it bobbed around in the muddy water. Will knew the vengeance of the river. No one need tell him, or any of the people who lived along its banks, that it was time to leave. They left quietly when it threatened.

By noon the rain had stopped and the sun broke through the clouds that were blowing swiftly to the East. Vulpes had taken the five pups up to the woodlot on the hill above the river bottom, and had trotted back to search for the others.

Meanwhile, Procyon awoke to find the river surging just below his hole in the sycamore. He put his head out and was frightened to see the water boiling beneath his door. Carefully he eased his way forward and climbed farther up the big tree. High in the slim branches he clutched eagerly to the swaying tree. Everywhere he looked he saw water. He was wet and uncomfortable and searched frantically for some route that would lead him to safety.

Suddenly, he felt the tree groan under the terrific force of the water. The ground had washed out from under it and it clung to the bank by a few tenacious roots. The giant sycamore danced like a toothpick in the vicious current. Procyon looked about fearfully. There was no escape. The tree was entirely surrounded by water, and the nearest limb of the next tree was just out of reach. He clung hopefully to his slim perch. Then, a roaring swell hit the tree and lifted it like a leaf from its mooring. The current twisted it gently and carried it out into the swift water. Procyon crawled to the higher branches that still jutted out of the river. The coon and the tree rode the rapid current like a swift ship. Then they hit a whirlpool and the great sycamore went down like a twig. The frightened Procyon was swallowed in the muddy flood. He was a strong and powerful swimmer and as he was carried away he made a bold attempt to save his life. However, the ground-hogs that had sought refuge in the high limbs of the leaning trees were unable to cope with the current when their havens were swept away. They went down with the flood.

Vulpes raced back along the high ridges of the hills above Muddy Branch. They were small islands jutting above the water. The fox saw no trace of his mate or youngsters. For several hours he wandered the deserted hills. Even the birds had left and flown inland where they could get more food. Trees, marking the bank of the old river bed were snapped one by one from their moorings as though they were twigs. Vulpes recognized nothing. All his trails were under water, and the familiar landmarks were gone. He took the ridge to the Queen farm, running swiftly, zig-zagging around the land to be sure he had not overlooked a spot where Fulva might be. The water was over the road now, and the scene around him was ugly in the light of the sun that burst the clouds.

Fulva was not on the hilltop. Vulpes searched vainly, glancing down on the farm scene below as he continued his anxious hunt. The Queen household was still busy. The water had come up to the pigpen and was lapping the fence around it. Through the trees Vulpes could see men rowing in boats as they picked chairs and chickens out of the flood. They looked strange and comic floating in the high branches of the oaks and poplars.

Vulpes ran down the hillside and into the valley once more. The brook below was a giant stream, boiling and carving itself a new bed in the soft black loam. He heard a whimpering. Looking to the right

Vulpes saw one of his pups preparing to leap the broad stream. He would crouch to spring, lose his nerve and then whine and wander back up the hill. Gathering up nerve again he would come back to the stream to jump. Vulpes ran over to him eagerly as the pup rushed toward him. The fox looked around for Fulva. The hill they were on was now an island, and he knew that if any of his family were stranded on it, they would soon die from lack of food. He skirted the land but found nothing. Vulpes came back to his cub and, without hesitating, ran for the stream, leapt and cleared the bank by several feet. The pup, inspired by his father's confidence, jumped after him. He made it safely and glided up the hill to the woodlot where his brothers and sisters were gathered.

As Vulpes brought his son to the woods, he stopped and sniffed the air. Fulva was coming downwind. Then he saw her with the other three cubs crossing the top of the hill. He barked and she stopped in her travels. Joyfully she ran to her mate. Fulva had led the other cubs out of the area by a circuitous route. The reunion was happy and the family capered in the drying leaves for several hours. Food was abundant. The mice and rabbits driven from their burrows and nests in the bottomlands

were now homeless strangers in the hills and easy prey for the woodland hunters.

The water reached its crest about sunset. Houses whipped downstream with the current like cracker boxes. All night long the river surged and strained. Then it started back to its bed. It dropped rapidly and by dawn the next day the roof tops of the houses along the canal had come back into view. They dripped with foul-smelling slimy mud.

Will Stack's house had been completely submerged but now he could see his chimney jutting above the water. He had moved in with Cy Cummings whose fields were covered with water but whose house stood high and dry on a hill above the flood. All the next day Will waited for the water to recede. That night the little shack stood ankle deep in calm muddy flood water, but his shed was gone. The current had torn it loose and tossed it down the river.

It took several more days for the river to drain to its normal bed. When it did, the stranded families along the waterfront trekked back like refugees to their sodden homes. They worked all week scooping the mud from their floors and washing the walls and furniture.

Mrs. Violet's home had suffered the most. The porch was caught in the trees that surrounded her place, and the front of the house had sagged and caved in. Her friends told her of the damage and advised her to move farther up the canal to an old lock house at Seneca Creek that had withstood the flood. The little old lady left her land, shaking her fist at the river and denouncing it loudly. Her brown, peaked hat bobbed with each accusation.

The men moved back but the foxes did not. Their hunting land was now covered with about an inch of sticky mud, and there was little or no food to be found in the Muddy Branch area.

Gradually the family broke up. Had it not been for the flood and had the foxes remained in their familiar haunts around Muddy Branch, the family would have been together longer. But with no den or cave to go to, the young foxes had roamed freely in this upland region. They had scattered gradually across the fields and hills, and when they did not come back, Vulpes knew that they had severed family ties to go off and live on their own.

Finally the last pup left them and Vulpes and Fulva were alone. In October they returned to Muddy Branch. Several rains had pounded the mud into the ground, and the falling autumn leaves had covered the sediment. Slowly the woodland returned to normal. Only the clusters of driftwood high in the trees, and an occasional plank in the beech limbs reminded them of the flood that had covered the land. Life went on where it had left off a month before.

CHAPTER NINE

The summer was gone and the winds were blowing colder. Cy Cummings had shocked his corn and the ears were stowed in the crib. His wheat was in and now that most of the hard summer work was done, he spent his time in the fields and woods, doing odd chores. One day when the air was brisk and fresh and the leaves were falling, Cy was out in the field mending a fence. He worked hard for several hours. The sweat stood out on his head and his back muscles grew stiff from bending over. He rose from his job and wiped his forehead with his big blue handkerchief. Cy stretched his back and looked up at the sky. The clouds were clean and white against the vivid blue, and the gold trimmings of the trees at the horizon sparkled and gleamed in the sunlight. High, high in the air the honk of geese caught his

attention. He squinted into the light and saw the V pattern of the wild geese flying south.

The old farmer stood still and watched them until they disappeared, honking faintly along their aerial highway. He smiled to himself, for as many times as he had seen the sight repeated each year, Cy never failed to respond to the thrill of the migrating birds. They meant the months of labor in the fields were done, that the autumn had come, the hunting season was opening, that the apples were red, and that the nuts were ripening on the trees. Cy leaned against the post and smelled the clean air. Presently he heard footsteps coming through the woods and turned to see the slightly stooped form of Will Stacks.

"Hello there," he called. "Mighty fine day, isn't it?"

" 'Deed it is, Cy," answered Will from the brightly splattered woodland. He walked over to meet his friend. Cy saw he had his trapping basket with him.

"Opening the season so soon?" he asked.

"No, thought I'd set out a few traps for mice and other varmints to see if there's any food left down there after the flood for the foxes and other critters. If there's food, there'll be foxes."

"Just saw some wild geese go by," Cy told the trapper.

"I heard 'em myself," he said, looking into the clouds. "I sure love those birds. Yes, sir, I love to see 'em pass. They make me sad and glad all at once."

"They usually stop by on the farm a little later in the season and fill up on corn," Cy said, looking at the sky where the birds had been.

"Yes," answered Will, "I've seen 'em out on that cornfield many a fall."

"Beautiful birds, too," Cy added. "Big beautiful birds." He seemed to be looking through the clouds now. Then he dropped his head and slapped the fence post. "Got to finish patching this thing today. It's been worrying me all summer." He bent down on his knees and went back to work with the plyers and mending wire. Stacks watched him a few minutes and then turned toward the woods.

"Guess I'll head down to the river. Sorta wanted to see if that big old Vulpes was still around."

"He's a cunnin' fox," Cy answered. "See him every now and then at the edge of the fence here. I believe that was his den that Charlie and I found last spring. Like to think so anyway."

Will was already off through the woods, his keen eyes detecting the signs of animal life around him.

Meanwhile Fulva and Vulpes were relaxing on the hill above the Branch. The heat was gone from the sun and it was pleasant to stretch out in the light now and enjoy the leisurely days of autumn. Their big family was gone and the two foxes were alone again. It had been a hard year for them. Many trials had interrupted their life and the responsibility of feeding and caring for such a large family had been a strain. But now their work was done. It was still too early for hunts, so the foxes were resting and enjoying the riches of their valley. Food was not hard to find. The air was cool and the fruits of autumn were a pleasant relief to their diet.

The days passed into November. On a cold clear night Vulpes started out across the land on a wide exploration of the fields and farms to the north of

Muddy Branch. He traveled most of the night and at dawn sought the protection of a small woodlot. With his head resting on his big brush, he dozed fitfully until the light had flooded the farms below him and he could see the big red barns shining in the morning light.

The wind shifted at daybreak and carried the smells of the farm across the meadow to the fox. He caught the odor of hounds and horses and men. Vulpes lifted his head curiously and looked at the distant farm more closely. He could see the men moving about. Some were dressed in bright scarlet coats, and others were in brown and black. They were all leading their horses from the stables to the bright outdoors and mounting them with ease and loud halloos.

Vulpes had come to the hill above the Hunt Club of Maryland, where the Master of the Fox Hounds and his dawn party were preparing for a chase across the hills. The M.F.H. wore his scarlet coat and was organizing the ride when the fox caught their scent on the wind. All were dressed according to the rules of the sport. Those in "pinks" had ridden five seasons or more, and those in Ratcatchers and Black Coats were occasional riders to the hounds. After the party had assembled, thirty or forty Walker hounds were led from their kennels and the spectacular group left the barns and trotted down the road to the meadow.

Here is a new hunt, Vulpes thought as he watched the hounds and horses from his warm spot on the hillside. He was not sure that he wanted to take this chase, but the snappy air of autumn had awakened the spirit of the hunt in the fox and he thought of leading this pack off to the river.

As the horses and riders came over the meadow, toward the hill where Vulpes lay, the rumble of their hoofs shook the earth. Voices sounded clear and joyous as the members of the hunt club rode behind the weaving pack of hounds. The Huntsman, Harry Williams, led the party. Coming over the hill, Vulpes could hear him encouraging the dancing pack.

"Hi up there, git 'em, old boy, git 'em up!"

Slowly Vulpes rose from his warm covert and calculated the open lands and fence rows. He moved out into the wind and crossed to the other side of the knoll. The Whippers-in, aides to the Huntsman, were moving out to the right and left of the hounds trying to hold them into a pack, when Gunner, the big Walker, caught the scent of Vulpes.

The hound bayed. The Huntsman lifted his arm and called out with a ringing voice that sounded across the entire farmlands, "Halloa!"

The hunt was off. Far down on the other side of the hill, Vulpes heard the ringing voice of Harry Williams. He stopped his leisurely gait and looked back. The horses had jumped to the opening note of the hunt; they were running across the field, their manes flying. The hounds were coming ahead of them baying like a great melodious organ. The fox had never seen such a sight, nor heard such a loud chorus of hounds. Their voices rose as one. He watched horses, riders and hounds a minute longer, then turned and ran along the edge of the fence. Vulpes knew he could outrun these hounds in a short time, but he didn't like the open country he was in. He made an excellent target on the dark loam.

As he glided past the osage orange hedge, one of the members of the hunt caught sight of his bright orange shape and lifted his hat into the air. This sent a chill of excitement through the galloping party and they thundered down the hill shouting, their red and black coats flashing in the morning light.

As the hunt rode on, the fox warmed to the occasion. He leapt the fence and darted through a glade of trees that ran along the stream bed. With a swift jump he cleared the water and glided out to the long, sloping meadow beyond. The hounds were in full voice now and their hymn resounded across the bright autumn landscape.

He heard them at the creek as he reached the knoll of the next hill, and stopped. Vulpes could not understand the purpose of this chase. They did not stalk him or lie in wait for him as Buck Queen did; they rode swiftly after him, spurring their horses to the race.

Vulpes passed through a woodlot and sped off across the field beyond. Far down the valley he listened to the hunt. The riders had come to the barrier of thick trees and were circling it on their horses. Only the Huntsman and the Whippers-in kept up with the hounds as they bayed through the saplings and darted out of the woods on the other side.

Again the fox heard the thundering pound of hoofs as the party reorganized and rolled across the field he had crossed. As Vulpes walked along he saw a herd of cattle grazing in the meadows just beyond. He was nervous in this open land and decided to lose the hunt by circling the herd and starting back to Muddy Branch.

He sped lightly past the ruminating animals, cut to the right and ran along the top of the fence at the edge of the field. With a spurt Vulpes was off and drifting swiftly back across the plowed land to the distant thickets of the river.

The hunt drew to a halt before the cattle. The Walkers lost the trail among the strong odors of the herd and were circling blindly over the field. The huntsman and the Whippers-in had reined their steeds and were calling the dogs back. The hunt was over. The scarlet riders turned their horses toward the kennels and trotted back across the fields and jumps.

As Vulpes came to Muddy Branch, he stopped and looked back across the hills. There was no sign of the hunters or hounds. He had left them miles behind in the rolling Maryland farmlands. The fox walked slowly back along an old quail avenue to the laurel slick. Fulva had just returned from a hunt for food and she was napping in the high noon shadows and lights.

Vulpes went down to the stream, lapped up the cold water, now black with leaves, and set out for the field to find some apples and berries. Under the knotty trees in an abandoned orchard he found many apples to gnaw on, and filled himself on the fruit until he was stuffed and round.

That night he led Fulva on a merry race over the

stream bed, across fallen trees and up and down the tow-path. Fulva nipped at his feet as he frisked up the trail that led to the hill above Buck's place.

A light glowed in the kitchen window sending a clean shaft of color out onto the frozen ground. Buck's wife, May, was crating the eggs she had gathered that day for market. She worked around the kitchen quietly and swiftly, unaware of the nocturnal visitors outside who were watching the shadows come and go.

There was a knock at the door. May put down her eggs and went to open it. The light from the kitchen streamed out into the starry November night. The dogs howled and pulled at their chains.

"Hello, Mr. Gordon," May said as she recognized the young man who owned a summer cottage next door. "Come in."

"Thank you," Gordon said as he entered.

"Hush, Fritz," May called to one of the dogs. "They're awfully restless tonight. Buck is in the parlor with some friends. Just step in and make yourself comfortable. I'll take your coat."

Gordon strolled across the Congoleum-covered floor to the parlor where four men were sitting around the kerosene stove.

"Hello there, Mr. Gordon," Buck called when he

recognized the tall, well-groomed neighbor. "Mr. Gordon, these are some friends of mine, Cy Cummings, Charlie Craggett and Will Stacks."

Gordon shook their hands and walked over to the

couch to sit down between Cy Cummings and Will Stacks. He glanced around the room as he took his place on a stool. Two lighted kerosene lamps stood on an oilcloth-covered table under the front window. The mantel held a small weather vane—a cottage that housed a witch and two children. The children were out, indicating fair weather. Newspaper clippings of foxes and dogs were tacked on the walls. Dotted swiss curtains hung across the windows. Over one window Joe noticed a large hole in the wall. Buck followed his gaze and commented as he crossed his legs:

"Suppose you're wondering about that hole up there, Mr. Gordon? May did that the other day when she picked up a .410 and took a shot at a mouse that was running across the curtain rod." He chuckled as he continued, "She missed the mouse but she certainly tore up the top of that window."

"A .410!" said Gordon in amazement.

"Yes, sir, a little old .410 did that—loaded with bird shot, too. If she had used my 12 gauge here," he motioned to the Long Tom that leaned against the wall behind his chair, "it would have been a lot bigger. I just wouldn't be afraid of going up against anything with a shotgun. If a man is steady enough and can hold his fire until fifteen feet, he'll be able to knock down most anything. Now, mind you, I'm not saying fifteen yards, I'm saying fifteen feet. Try it for yourself sometime."

"You'd certainly have to be steady," Gordon declared.

"That you do, Mr. Gordon," said Charlie Craggett, "and you won't find a steadier one than old Buck Queen. I remember the time that we were out hunting and a fox was coming right down the trail toward us. Buck called to that fox to make him turn so he could get a side shot and not spoil the fur. There ain't many men that can call their shots like that, Mr. Gordon."

Buck chuckled, "Charlie, I've done that a good many times, I'm not afraid of his getting away whatsoever, if he's within thirty to thirty-five yards of me." The old hunter spoke modestly—simply stating a fact.

"I gather that you've been hunting foxes a good many years," Jim Gordon observed.

"Well, I've been hunting most of my life."

"Are there many foxes around here, Mr. Queen?"

"I get about fifteen or twenty a year, and Will Stacks picks up more than that in his traps each season. There are still a lot around in spite of that, too. They were going to bring in the government fellows just to trap the foxes. Said they couldn't raise turkeys in the flats above.

"But there was a time when there weren't many. One night when I was a young man, that was well over forty years ago, I had some night hounds out to hunt coon, and those dogs just weren't behaving right. They didn't do a single thing they should have done. I couldn't figure out what had happened. That was right in Chevy Chase where you live now, Mr. Gordon. It wasn't built up then and was good hunting ground. I finally tracked the trouble down to a red fox that had got loose from the zoo in Washington. That was the first fox I ever hunted in these parts. We used to have to go miles and miles before we could start a fox in those days."

"Hmm, strange there wasn't any fox hunting around here in those days," said Gordon.

"Well, now, I reckon there was some, but foxes were scarce. However, there were places in Maryland and Virginia, a good many of the wealthy Washington people have hunted foxes through the years, just the way they do it in England. I'm told George Washington did a good bit of hunting in places not too far away before he got to be President.

"They had hunt clubs in those days just like they do now. The Old Dumblane Club, right near your home on Wisconsin Avenue in Washington, was a famous club. Those people liked to go on the hunt for the ride, however, and seldom killed a fox.

"I used to watch them ride out from town in big wagons they called Tallyhos, drawn by a fine set of matched bobtails. It was a mighty pretty sight—all the hunters dressed in red coats with shining boots and spurs; the hounds baying, the Huntsman blowing his horn. Many times they didn't chase a fox at all, but had their kennel man go out with a bag of anise seed and drag it over the jumps and across the open fields where the horses could go. Then they'd turn the hounds loose, and they would follow that trail as they'd been trained. It was an exciting thing to watch those people go over the fences and obstacles after the hounds. But they seldom came out here. This isn't good riding land—never has been. You just can't get through these dense woods on a horse. By the time the riders got around the thickets and wire fences, the fox would be miles and miles away. They wouldn't see much of the dogs on a race like that.

"But, it is a different story now. Foxes have become right plentiful."

Gordon wanted to know why the foxes had suddenly appeared in this land where such a short time ago there were none.

"Soon as you open up the land it seems to increase the food for them. Mice, rabbits and quail move in, and the foxes follow."

"Well, why is that?" asked Gordon. "I should think the farmers would kill them as soon as they came into their land."

"They are a cunnin' thing, now, Mr. Gordon, when you figure them out. Our American fox is a clever animal. He's hunted and trapped, and the only way he can survive is by his wits. Those that aren't smart enough won't live long. Living close to men and farms they learn to be tricky. You notice sometimes foxes that aren't hunted much are easy to knock down. The fox that lives around here—and you'll find that same fox on the outskirts of almost every town throughout this whole region and right on up into Canada—is a right smart animal. Stands to reason he's got to be a right cunnin' thing. He has no protection whatsoever. You can run him any time, take him any time. Lots of states even pay you a bounty if you kill him, and still he more than holds his own."

"The ideal country for a fox," Cy Cummings put in, "is a land where you have farms and woods both. Farms where they can hunt, and woods where they can seek shelter and raise their young."

"They're a great sport to hunt!" Will Stacks said as he shifted his position on the couch.

" 'Deed they are," Cy Cummings agreed. "One time when I was down in Virginia we went on a fox hunt that I'll never forget. An old red fox that lived in the hills was known to be smarter than a book. We thought we'd get him. Well, sir, about fifteen of us started out after that fox on horses with a pack of good hounds. We rode all day, from early morning, on his trail. We changed horses three times. Most of the men dropped out by night and all the hounds but two. Three of us decided to see it out, so we rested during the night while the dogs and fox carried on the hunt. Next morning we picked up the chase. By noon we ended the hunt. The hounds just gave out. That fox had broken a whole pack, wore out three relays of horses and nearly finished us. He was a wonderful animal."

"There is a fox right around here that's no fool," said Will. "Folks that know him call him Vulpes. He got out of one of my traps last winter, and you know, that fox won't even come near a trap that I've set since. He knows what I'm up to."

"Believe I've hunted that fox," said Buck. "Like to get him, too. Great, big, noble dog-fox, just a beautiful thing with the fullest fur I've ever seen. I saw him in Brushy Valley one time. He eluded the hounds that day by going down a creek bed. I think he was a first year fox, new to hunting when I saw him, but he's wise now. He learned enough on that first hunt to hold him over for a lifetime. Brownie

gets his trail a lot but he has never run him in. The fox is too smart for that."

Gordon was listening to the men with great interest when a low slurring yap sounded through the night.

"Sounds like Vulpes," said Buck, listening. "He calls to the dogs for a chase now and then."

"You mean he *wants* to be hunted?" asked Gordon.

"Yes, indeed, they'll challenge those dogs to a race. They absolutely will. Those foxes love a hunt and they aren't afraid of any dog. I've even seen and heard them bark on a chase. Now, lots of old timers say the dogs won't run a barking fox, but they will; I've seen them do it. Take a fox in good condition, give him a fair race, and he'll absolutely outrun them. Now, maybe if he's old, or a little sick, or he's just had a big meal, they might catch him, but even then he has to be in strange ground or he'll den. But not if he's in good condition, Mr. Gordon.

"He's not worried about those dogs as long as he has them behind him. You go out here anywhere after a light snow and you can find fox tracks within fifty yards of the house. Now, I've got a lot of hounds around here, and if he was really worried about those dogs—if they were going to catch him or anything—he'd leave here. Goes to show you a fox doesn't worry much about dogs.

"But," the old hunter went on, "if there is a whole lot of noise and people in the woods, and the fox knows there are a lot of hounds all scattered and running through the hills, that fox is going to leave.

Doesn't worry about those dogs, but he wants them behind him, not in front.

"I remember one time out in the woods I saw two foxes. One of the few times in my life I could have got a double shot at foxes. It was early March; their scent was very strong that day. Instead of going down the path, I was going through the woods. A fellow up here had some mean dogs and his place was posted. A man doesn't like to go on someone else's place and herd a dog with a stick or something, so I circled on through the woods around his land and came to a stream. I was just out listening to my hounds; I love to hear them run. I noticed a movement in the laurel. I saw it was a fox.

"The fox smelt and looked around, went down the stream and sat on a log. Another fox went over and curled up on a log and sniffed around, went down to get a drink of water, and came on back and curled up on the log. Curled up loose-like, like he wasn't going to sleep. He was only there a few minutes, then he got up and listened to the hounds. They were chasing still a third fox. When the hounds got close, those two foxes just moved over to the left in the ivy. The hounds passed within fifteen yards of where these foxes had been, chasing the other fox. Hounds went right on to Muddy Branch. After the dogs had passed, the two foxes

came right back to the log just as if they were used to such things—unconcerned as anything. Just got out of the way, and then came right on back."

"You mean they just went up into the laurel thicket and came right on back and didn't see you?"

"Sure. Course I had to be very quiet. A fox will trust his nose more than his ears or eyes. Take those two foxes I just told you about, they paid no attention to me even though I was in plain sight. But if they had caught just one whiff of my scent, they would have left there right pronto. I guess a fox doesn't reason like a man does, and if you stand real still and don't make any noise he figures you're just a part of the woods. The same thing is true for the gray fox. Last November I was out with Brownie and Joe. We were running that big red up on the hill, the same fox that Will was talking about, Vulpes. Well, sir, a gray fox came walking through the woods and crossed the trail right in front of me. He stood in the center of the trail listening to the hounds and never paid any attention to me."

"That's right, Buck," said Will Stacks. "Sometimes you can call a fox right over to you. I remember one time I was resting along the fence in the southwest corner of Charlie's pasture. I caught a glimpse of something moving through the laps lying in the woods just beyond the fence. It looked like a red fox, so I squeaked like a mouse to see what would happen. That fox turned and came bounding through the fence. I stayed very quiet. About fifty feet away the fox stopped and stood up on his hind feet to look over the tall grasses. Then I squeaked again and he ran closer. When he was only a few feet away, he watched me very carefully but didn't seem to be too scared. A gust of wind carried my scent to him and he got out of there in one big hurry." Old Will Stacks chuckled as he relived the incident.

Buck and the others laughed with him and for a moment the room was filled with their deep chuckles.

"They certainly can travel, can't they, Will, when they set their mind to it?" Buck said. "I can't help admiring them when I see them gliding through the woods just as smooth as can be. And then in a little while you see your hounds come scrambling through the woods chasing them, and those dogs are really working hard. Their legs are flying in all directions and they're huffing and puffing and look like they're going like the wind, but that old fox is way out ahead of them. I remember one time I brought one down as he was going across River Road. That fox didn't look like he was hurrying at all, but he was covering more than thirty feet with each bound. I fired when he was in the center of the road. There was a light snow on the ground and when I walked over to pick him up I found that he had never touched the road. He had taken off from one bank and even though I shot when he was midway across, he didn't come down until he was on the other side."

"I figure they can make nigh onto thirty miles an hour," added Charlie Craggett, "and that's good time for a horse."

"Yes it is, Charlie, but they can do it," said Cy.

"I clocked a red fox when he ran down River Road ahead of my car one night, and he was doing better than twenty-eight miles an hour."

"A red fox can do it, but a gray fox can't," said Buck. "Put the dogs on the trail of a gray fox and, given a fair chance, they will absolutely run him down."

"Is there that much difference between a gray and a red fox?" asked Gordon.

"Two different animals, Mr. Gordon. I'd like to

take you on a few fox hunts. Maybe we could get in a couple of good solid races, and then you'd see the difference between running a red and running a gray. For one thing, a red doesn't den much whereas a gray takes to a den or tree within a few hours."

"Why is that?"

"Doesn't have the speed and endurance of the red," answered Buck. "A red fox is way out ahead of those hounds, maybe a half mile or more, all the time. He's more cunning than a gray, but he doesn't cut capers until the dogs have run him awhile. On the other hand, the gray isn't so far ahead and he's doing everything he can to slow those dogs. If you follow his trail you can see that he runs for a dense thicket. This checks the hounds. When he leaves the thicket he might run along a log. Then he drops to the ground and starts running the laps. This breaks up his trail and makes it hard for the dogs to follow."

"I don't know what you mean by 'running the laps'," said Gordon.

"Well, sir," said Buck, "by laps I mean the tops of trees that are left lying in the woods when the trees are chopped down. Around these parts only the trunk of the tree is hauled away. The gray fox runs along these cut treetops, goes out on a big long limb, drops to the ground and then runs over to another lap and does the same thing all over again. A dog can't make any time following a trail like that. If he could he'd run that fox down in short order. As it is, they usually den or tree a gray if he doesn't get too far ahead of them."

"I didn't know they could climb trees."

"I've never seen a gray go up a big straight tree but I've found a good many that have gone up leaning trees. Yes, they can climb, but if they're hard pressed they usually den.

"There's an old woodchuck hole not a hundred yards away from the house right up there on the hill where I denned a gray fox just the other day. It was not a regular fox den but the dogs were right behind him and he had to take shelter."

"There certainly is a lot to learn in the woods. And right around here too, not thirty miles from Washington," reflected Gordon.

"To get all there is out of the woods you have to go out time after time," mused Buck. "You might think an animal never does a certain thing until one time you are right there, and you see him do it. Then you know he does it. Somebody else who has not seen what you have might doubt you but you know what you've seen."

"I suppose so," said Gordon, digging into his pocket for his knife. "You've probably seen things out here that few people have." Pulling at the blade he opened his knife and began to whittle on a stray stick.

Charlie Craggett and Will Stacks were half listening to Buck and half dreaming. Will was thinking about the things he had seen in the woods that no one would believe. Strange happenings among the animals that he had never told to anyone because he knew they would not take him seriously. He well knew what Buck meant, and he also knew that Gordon would never understand.

"Why is it that three times out of five, on the average," Buck was saying to the young man, "a man will knock down a fox and cripple him bad and the dogs will fail to run him from there?" Will Stacks pieced together the conversation he had missed while dreaming and concluded that Buck must be telling Gordon about some of the mysteries of the wild.

"That's what I want to know," said Buck, scratching his forehead. "As well as I know dogs, I can't unriddle that. I've tried my best. I've had it happen time and time again. Joe out there stopped a chase one day after I had wounded a fox, and just wouldn't go on. I told him to hunt him up . . . but nothing doing. He just turned around and went home. I searched that place till I liked to wear it out and came back the next day to search again. I hunted and hunted and hunted, but I never did find that fox. On the other hand, I've had the dogs run 'em down in a hundred yards."

For a moment there was a silence among all the men. Stacks was staring at the flickering coal oil flame, and Buck was shaking his head slowly, thinking over the many, many incidents that had filled his life along the river.

May Queen came into the room with a hot drink and asked the men if they would have some.

"Brownie is pretty restless tonight," she said to Buck. "I believe that old Vulpes has been out there on the hill this evening."

"Should leave a pretty fresh trail out there," said Will.

"Probably be playing around on the hill all night," said Buck. "Old Vulpes loves that hill. Comes back time and time again. Joe or Brownie will pick up his trail in the bottoms and zoommm . . . they'll go right up the hill after him."

"Do you think we could get him, if we went out?" asked Jim enthusiastically.

"Maybe in the morning," said Buck. "Not tonight."

The men sipped their hot drink in silence. Buck was blowing on the brew and thinking about Vulpes.

Stacks swallowed loudly: "There's not much chance of my getting him. He's wise to me."

"Mr. Queen was telling me one day that you lure foxes with a brew you make," said Gordon. "Is it difficult to mix?"

Old Will smiled and put the chipped cup down on his saucer.

"Sure is, young man, sure is."

"Well, how is it done, Mr. Stacks?"

"Now, that is something I wouldn't even tell old Buck over here. It's a secret. The only real secret I have. If I let that out I sure would have everyone taking my livelihood away from me." The man laughed softly and looked at the smooth face of young Gordon. "That I cannot tell you. But I could tell you some other things like tanning or where and how to trap. Anything else, Mr. Gordon, anything else but that."

Gordon looked at the man. He suddenly realized that he was not talking to an ignorant old river dweller. Here were men who were experts at their trade. For a moment the young man was embarrassed. There was much that he would never know. These men were craftsmen. In a sense they had their own patents. The knowledge they had gathered and the exact methods by which they applied it had become an art. Gordon felt only great respect.

Jim Gordon looked at their tanned faces and sensed their robust independence. Here were men who punched no time clock, who reported to work only at the dictation of the sun and rain. The work they did was a way of life they enjoyed. Gordon thought for a moment of how he worked all year to spend a vacation at his farm on the Potomac River. These men spent their lives at what he called a vacation. He turned to look at Will Stacks.

"How do you handle your trapped animals, Mr. Stacks?" he heard himself saying.

Stacks rubbed his hands together and looked at the man.

"When I take a fox from a trap, I do it as quick as I can and use gloves so that my own scent won't linger around the site. If I do it right, that trap is better than ever. The scent of the fox around the spot helps to attract other foxes. Sometimes I've caught several foxes the same night in one set.

"I usually skin them right out in the woods so I won't have to carry them home. When I get all the flesh removed from the hide, I take the pelt and put it on a drying board. That's about all I do. Sell them just that way. Round here you might get anywhere from five to ten dollars for a pelt—good prime pelt.

"Now, if I were to want a pelt for myself I would have to tan it. The hide is very thin on a fox so it tans easily. I soak it thoroughly in water and then I wash it well in soapy water with maybe a little soda or borax in it. Make sure it's good and clean. If it's still a little greasy I rinse it in gasoline.

"There are a couple of methods of tanning. I usually take about a quart of table salt, some sulphuric acid and mix it in a bucket of water. Put the pelt in that a few days. Then take it out. Rinse it in a bucket of water and soda. This gets all the acid out of it and makes it clean. After that I work it dry." Stacks demonstrated with his big hands how he pulled the pelt apart, stretched and crumpled it.

"Tack it on a board to dry and work a little Neatsfoot oil into it when it is nearly dry. And that is all there is to it. It's not hard to tan a hide, Mr. Gordon."

Gordon was not convinced.

"I would like to see you do that sometime," he said finally, after thinking it over.

"Come by any time in the fall," said Stacks, "and I'll be glad to show you."

"The missus sure likes that fur you tanned for her, Will," said Cy. "It's a fox that came down to my chicken pen years ago before I cooped them all up," he explained to Gordon.

"Do these foxes get a lot of your chickens?"

asked Gordon. "That's the only thing I've heard they eat."

Charlie Craggett, who had been sitting quietly, answered the question.

"Sure, they'll take chickens, especially in the spring when the vixens are nursing. But they don't get them if you coop them up. However, if you let them run around all night, like some of those squatters do along River Road, 'course they'd get a few. But they don't get any if you take care of them right."

"That's just the way I feel about it, Charlie," said Buck. "A fox'll eat what he can get. I guess about the easiest and most abundant food around here would be mice of one sort or another. I figure mice and rabbits is what a fox lives on. 'Course he might take a quail now and then, especially if there are a lot of them around. And he eats insects, grasshoppers and crickets. He'll even eat fruit like apples and cherries and blackberries. He eats a surprising amount of fruit. But a fox is primarily a meat-eating animal, and he can't get along without it."

The hours had passed rapidly without the men realizing it. Gordon looked at his watch and decided he had better get along home.

"I tell you what, Mr. Gordon," Buck said. "If you

would like to go on a fox hunt, I think it'll be pretty good tomorrow."

The young man looked up, beaming.

"I'd like that, Mr. Queen," he agreed eagerly.

"Let's try that old Vulpes," said Stacks.

"He makes a good chase," Cy Cummings added.

"Well," said Buck Queen, "we can try. But you're sure picking a hard one if you want to run him."

"He sounds wonderful," Gordon said, smiling broadly. "What time shall I be here?"

"We'd better go out early in the morning when the trails are still fresh," Buck answered. "Foxes don't move around much during the day, and it's hard for the dogs to pick up a scent then."

"How early, Mr. Queen? This'll be one time I won't mind hearing the alarm go off." The men laughed.

"Well, let's see, the sun comes up about seven now. I guess seven thirty would be early enough."

"Think I'll come along," said Charlie. "Like to see that fox myself."

"Count me in," Cy added.

"All right," said Buck. "We'll all go, and it'll be a hunt that you've never seen the like of before. 'Cause if we're hunting Vulpes, I can tell you it won't be just a jaunt in the woods. It may last days."

"If it does," said Gordon, rising and reaching for his coat, "I'm going to call the office and tell them I won't be in. I'm sick of that desk anyway."

One by one the men got up and put their coats on. They were all excited by the thought of the hunt and the house emptied quickly. The dogs barked loudly as they left.

As Gordon walked down the road to his farm, his steps were light. He pictured himself raising his shotgun and getting the fox that had gained the admiration of all the men who lived along the river.

CHAPTER TEN

Vulpes and Fulva were running over the bottomlands and hills of Muddy Branch when the men left Buck's parlor. Starlight twinkled brightly through the bare limbs of the trees, and the foxes found the cold damp trails exciting and full of interest. They led to pools where the ice was forming. Sharp crisp notes sang through the quiet hills as the ice closed in against the bank. Rabbits were nibbling roots and digging for fruits under the dark loam. A screech owl quivered from his perch low in a pine tree. His feathers stood out from his body in a puffy circle, his head pivoted freely and swiftly on his shoulderless body as he surveyed the night life below him.

Around midnight, Fulva wandered back to the laurel slick above Muddy Branch to curl up under the smooth glossy leaves. As she dozed off to sleep she could hear Blarina, the shrew, tunneling under the earth. In the silent darkness his subterranean explorations sounded as though he were uprooting the whole earth.

After Fulva left him, Vulpes turned to the high lands and trotted easily from ridge to ridge. The cold freeze of winter had brought renewed vigor to the fox and with this bubbling restless energy coursing through him, he was anxious to be off through the forests, following the wild instincts within him to live and match his wits against his enemies and prey of the fields and river. It was just dawn when he left the hills and crossed through the bottom-lands below Buck's farm to return to the laurel thicket where Fulva was sleeping. He curled up at the other end of the brush and closed his eyes as the sun touched the gray tops of the sycamores and poplars. The light streamed across the Potomac River and sketched long shadows to the west of the Maryland trees.

Half an hour earlier Gordon's alarm clock went off and the young man awoke to stretch, and yawn as he rubbed his eyes. He remembered the hunt and ran from his bunk to dress in the shivering cold.

Over on River Road Will Stacks was already up. He was dressing warmly for he knew he would need plenty of covering before the hunt was done.

Cy Cummings had built a fire in the wood stove in his kitchen and was finishing breakfast before he went out to start his car.

Charlie Craggett was crossing the fields to Cy's house. His breath crystallized into white clouds as he thumped across the frozen furrows.

Buck Queen had eaten breakfast and was out in the backyard with his dogs. He had his morning chores to finish before the hunt.

Just at dawn Cy's car bounced up the corduroy road to the gate. Buck could hear the wheezing motor of Will's car on the feeder road. He followed its progress in the quiet morning. The noise carried distinctly across the hill. Jim Gordon was coming around the bend in the road, running to keep the cold out of his bones.

As the men gathered all were anticipating the hunt that lay ahead of them this day. Their guns were greased and in order. The vision of the princely red fox ran through each man's mind. He was lined along the sights of Cy's shotgun, and Will's shotgun, and Charlie's shotgun and Jim's.

The frosted air sent the blood tingling through their veins and each hunter knew that this was his day. The weather promised to be clear and cold. No winds were blowing.

The five men gathered in Buck's kitchen and enjoyed the steaming drink that had been prepared for them before starting along the trails. They left silently, buttoning their jackets tightly around their necks. There was little talk. Stacks checked his pockets to make sure he had sufficient ammunition. Jim slung his gun over his shoulder and looked across the farm to the shadowy hills beyond. Somewhere among the trees and bushes lay Vulpes, the Red Fox.

Buck released Brownie and Joe. They loped through the yard sensing the excitement in the waiting men. Brownie hit the road and dropped his head to smell the cold frosted earth. Joe followed closely on his heels. The hounds ran nervously from one side of the road to the other. The men closed in behind.

The Red Bone left the road a short distance from the house and slid through the brush and honeysuckle of the bottom lands. He held his nose close to the ground as he traveled. Then he crossed the trail that Vulpes had taken as he returned to the laurel slick. The hound's voice rang out. He caught the scent again, and another deep note sounded through the silent hills.

As he followed the cold trail to the hill his tones became more excited.

"They're on a trail," Buck said quietly to the

men. "Let's go up the ravine and take stations on the hills."

Vulpes raised his head as he heard the hounds top the hill. They were still far away. He did not know whose trail they might be following. As the dogs dropped into the valley and their voices were lost between the hills, Vulpes put his head down again. But he was curled loosely, and was ready to leap at the first alarm. He heard the hounds once more. This time they were much closer. The fox rose to his feet. He listened to their course in the still woods and knew they were coming his way. He waited until Brownie and Joe came down the hill a quarter of a mile beyond and then trotted out of the thicket. Now he knew the Red Bone and the Blue Tick hound had found his trail. The first hunt of the season was on. Vulpes turned away and drifted easily from the laurel patch.

The fox was full of life and vigor this crisp autumn morning and quickly gathered speed until he was sprinting down the hill before the baying of the hounds. Brownie picked up his fresh trail at the edge of the laurel thicket and the tone of his voice changed. It was excited and sharper. He had hit the new warm trail and knew he had roused Vulpes. Joe was close behind him. Vulpes had led the dogs safely away from Fulva, who was still resting on the hill. She lifted her head as the hounds went past the far end of the ivy patch and watched them go down over the hill toward the stream where Vulpes had just been. They came within fifty yards of her.

Far behind, uphill from the road, the party of hunters were standing on a knoll, waiting anxiously to catch the sound of the hounds. Then they heard the voice of Joe. It came ringing plaintively across the hills, rising from the river bottoms.

"They've headed down toward Muddy Branch," said Buck. He motioned to the men to follow him across the top of the hill and out to an old lumber road that led through the woods.

"Guess we'd better get to our stations. They'll be circling back before long." In single file the men walked quietly through the valley, across a swampy little stream and climbed the next hill.

"Gordon, you stand on that hill by the fence. Watch that field. He'll probably go down that fence line." Gordon draped his gun through his arm and pushed up the trail. The climb was steep and he was glad to make the top. He sat down on the nearest log and looked around. Not a twig was stirring. A few crows flew over the field and he aimed his gun at them.

"Bang! I sure would have gotten them," the young man mused proudly. He watched the field as Buck had told him to do. He could hear the rest of the party stealing over the dry leaves to their posts. They seemed far away. Gordon looked at the field again. It was silent and uninteresting. He looked down at an acorn at his feet. It had been chewed empty by a squirrel. Then he remembered he must look at the field. Hours seemed to pass and still the young man neither heard the dogs nor saw the fox. He wondered how much longer he could sit on the cold uncomfortable stump. Gordon shifted his position to lodge himself more comfortably between the uneven slivers of wood. Then he looked up at the field.

Meanwhile, down in Muddy Branch Vulpes was standing on a log with his head cocked to one side. He had dashed ahead of the hounds and was waiting for them to come within earshot. High above him a squirrel, disturbed by the fox's presence, was chattering at him from his limb. The fox looked up at him, blinked as if bored, and glanced back through the woods in the direction of his pursuers.

The mellow notes of the hounds rang out. The great fox turned and walked slowly along the woodland floor and circled back toward them. As their baying became louder and louder, Vulpes slid behind a log and watched them pass not one hundred yards away.

Brownie's nose was high now. He was intently following the trail and did not see the fox watching him from the covert. The wind was blowing toward Vulpes. The smell of hounds came to him. He sniffed, watched them take his circling trail into the woods, and then moved on. His route took him back to the laurel patch where he had left Fulva. She had smelt him approaching and was coming down the hill toward him. Vulpes thought about the race and was worried to see his mate. The dogs might pick up her trail if they met, and start out after her. Swiftly, he dashed and wheeled into the slick.

The booming voice of the Red Bone suddenly alerted the vixen and she bounded forward. Right over the hills before the hounds she sped. Her path led toward the hunting party. Vulpes waited. He heard Brownie hesitate a moment where the two trails met. His cry became confused. Before he could check the speed of his advance which carried him along, he caught Fulva's warm trail and was off. Vulpes lay down and listened to the hunt.

Fulva ran along the ridges and slipped through the brush and thickets wherever she could. She was pleased to find she could keep so far ahead of the dogs. Fulva had discovered the joy of the hunt and the pleasures of leading the singing hounds over the hills and valleys. She sprinted ahead, threading her way around the trees and over the rocks. The lovely vixen jumped from stone to stone in the creek bottoms and then waited on the other side of a hill to hear the Red Bone come to the water's edge and run in circles as he sought her lost scent.

At the crest of the next hill she stopped. An open field lay in her path. This was one of her favorite hunting areas. She turned swiftly and ran down the fence row. Gordon was not fifty feet away. He had just dropped his eyes to look at the acorn at his feet. The vixen checked her run when she caught the scent of the man. She was about to turn back, but the distant cry of the hounds pressed her forward. The red fox wound through the bushes and grasses that hugged the fence and darted silently past the hunter. She did not turn a twig. When she was just beyond his view she left the fence, cut into the woods, circled the knoll on which he was sitting, below his line of vision, and sprinted back to Muddy Branch. She took the rocky ridges where her trail would be hard to follow.

As she covered the miles to the Branch, Joe and Brownie burst out of the woods and whipped down the fence row past Gordon. The young man looked up. Joe saw him sitting close to the trail and wagged his tail happily. He had brought the fox to the hunter.

Then Gordon knew what had happened. The fox had passed in front of him and he had not seen it. The young man jumped to his feet and with great embarrassment trained his eyes on the field. But it was too late. He watched the dogs practically circle his feet as they followed the scent of Fulva. He moaned painfully. He had missed his big chance to bring down the clever fox.

Buck heard the hounds close in on the fence rail. He waited to hear the shot that would end the hunt. Cy Cummings from his station was also following the progress of the fox and hounds and he, too, looked toward the hill where Gordon stood. All was quiet.

Gordon was running after the hounds as they circled the hill. He snapped the safety on his gun and stood poised and ready; but there was nothing in

sight. Only the motionless trees and the dry leaves of the oaks still clinging to the limbs. He heard Buck coming over the path toward him.

"Looks like he went right by," said the old hunter when he was within earshot of the young man.

"I sure didn't see a thing," Gordon said meekly.

"You have to watch close. Can't drop your eyes a minute or they'll slip right by. They're way ahead of the dogs."

Gordon hooked his gun under his arm and followed Buck silently. He had nothing to say. The hounds had done their part, but he had not been ready. Old Buck Queen was smiling as he led the young man along. He enjoyed seeing the clever animals outwit the hunters.

"That fox has wind of us now," he said presently. "He'll head down to Muddy Branch again. Guess we'd better move on. He won't come back here."

From out of the glades and dusky trees and vines, the other hunters came. Will seemed to come from the side of a tree like a piece of bark. If he had not moved Gordon would not have seen him at all. Cy left his thicket of spice bushes. It was as if part of the woods had moved away. Jim Gordon realized he was a novice in the art of stalking prey.

Fulva cut sharply to the left of the path she was following and reached the laurel slick. Vulpes was waiting for her. He was glad to see her coming down through the autumn landscape, her brushy tail held straight out behind her. She was coming swiftly, and Vulpes sensed the fear in her anxious steps. He knew this was not a hunt to exercise the dogs. Fulva had seen men. He waited until she reached his side. The big fox looked down at his mate and nudged her gently. Then he carefully started off along her footsteps. At the crest of the hill he turned and disappeared into the woods. Fulva watched him go. She walked far back into the dense protective leaves and curled up quietly.

Vulpes was leading the chase now. He walked slowly so that when the hounds came to the crossing of the two trails his would be the fresher and easier to follow. The woods and hills lay before him, cold and shining in the sunlight. Through the trees he could see the river gleaming. Chipmunks left their seeds and nuts and scurried to the branches above as the big fox moved forward. He ignored their frantic efforts to escape him. Vulpes was listening to Brownie, his voice rising and falling as he covered the rolling woodlands. The deep lugubrious cry of Joe punctuated the song of the Red Bone. The hunt was fierce and earnest. Vulpes glided down to the waters of Muddy Branch excited and thrilled with the chase. He felt no fear.

The hounds had followed Fulva's trail to the fork. They never hesitated as they dashed along the path she had followed. Immediately they picked up the fresh scent of Vulpes and ran down the hill toward the stream where he stood.

The fox followed the slowly winding water to the canal. He looked the situation over a moment and then decided what he would do. The stream went under the canal at this point. Engineers had funneled it beneath the waterway in a large stone aqueduct. The fox slipped along the ledge at the side of the tunnel and ran out the other end. He clambered up the bank on the opposite side and raced up the tow-path. Half a mile up the canal he caught the scent of a mouse in the grasses nearby. Vulpes quietly stalked him and dined in the long grasses while Brownie and Joe worked out the puzzle at the foot of the stream.

The old Red Bone reached the canal bank and swerved to follow it. The intriguing patterns that Vulpes left in the leaves and streams for him to solve would have baffled the ordinary hound. But Brownie had not become a lead hound and the pride of old Buck Queen for nothing. He worked out the problems of the trail with almost human wisdom. Skillfully and methodically he covered the probable route Vulpes had taken. Finding nothing, he returned to the edge of the aqueduct where he had lost the trail. Once more he went over the fox's course. Joe was still working the near-by woods and the top of the canal bank. Brownie went down to the edge of the stream. Picking his feet high he

waded the cold, shallow waters and sniffed the air of
the tunnel. Suddenly he caught a faint wisp of the
fox odor. He traced it to the ledge that ran along the
inside of the arching wall. His loud, long cry told Joe
he had at last found the lost trail. Joe raced to the
stream, splashed through the shallows and sped
through the tunnel beneath the canal. As he burst
into the sunlight on the other side of the canal
Brownie had already climbed to the tow-path.

Joe sprinted up the hill after the Red Bone who
had found the fresh trail leading up the path.

Vulpes had finished his meal. He pricked up his
ears when he heard the hounds on the path. He

knew they had worked out his trail and even as he heard their piercing cries he rose and trotted off. About a quarter of a mile farther, he crossed the canal again, this time on the Violet Locks, and climbed up the rocks to the hills. From the rocky blasted precipice high above the waterway he could see far down the tow-path. There were Brownie and Joe, their heads high as they bayed into the wind. The fox pranced and crouched in the leaves as he watched them coming along the opposite shore of the canal and then turned to trot away over the rocky cliffs.

Suddenly Vulpes stopped. A twig snapped in the woods to the left of him. The leaves were rustling strangely. His sharp ears caught the sound of heavy footsteps. Vulpes knew the hunters were around him. He stepped around a rock and tried to pass the men. The fox was picking his way cautiously ahead when a slight movement by the base of a poplar tree caught his attention. He turned his head quickly and detected the motionless form of Will Stacks. The man was not moving a muscle. Vulpes watched him for some minutes trying to be sure the brown figure was not just part of the trees and forest. He was certain he had seen movement. Then Will Stacks put his hand to his face. He rubbed a wheal on his cheek where a twig had stung him. With that movement the man took shape for Vulpes. He saw the hunter clearly. Swiftly he darted below the rim of the hill and dashed along the slippery rocks. When he had put several hills between himself and the hunter, Vulpes decided to leave the country. The woods were full of men.

It was almost noon now. The hunt had been going steadily since daybreak. All told the chase had covered almost thirty miles. It had been a fast exciting chase, for the cool weather had enabled the hounds to hold to the trail. Now, however, the warmth of noon had thawed the frost and the body scent was riding higher in the air, making it more difficult for the hounds to follow. Vulpes was ready to make a break across the country.

He ran out onto the road that led to Buck's place and suddenly turned in his tracks. The fox walked back on his own trail. When he had gone about one hundred yards he made a running leap that cleared the bank and carried him well up the hillside in one easy motion. He bounded up through the woodlot to River Road and the farms and fields beyond.

Brownie and Joe were beginning to feel the strain of the many miles they had covered that day. They slowed down at the bluffs but they did not stop.

Buck called to them, encouraging them to bring in the fox, and they loped off toward the road, saving their energy for the long miles still ahead.

Suddenly the trail disappeared again. But Brownie knew this trick. He wove back and forth along the road, back tracking until he came to the spot where Vulpes had leapt. Then he circled the area in a wider and wider arc. Joe was dashing from fence to fence, trying to discover which way the fox had jumped. Then both hounds broke into full cry. They had found where the fox had landed and darted through the fence to the hills. They were off again.

Buck noticed the change in the hounds' direction and stopped his trek to Muddy Branch.

"They're going out to River Road," he called to his companions. "If we cut across the glen here and get up on that hill we might see him before he gets too far." The men turned and followed the chase. The voice of the hounds rang out clearly now. They had caught their second wind and the hunt was once more in full swing.

Vulpes ran down River Road leisurely. He stopped frequently to locate the dogs. He sensed their renewed vigor. Old Brownie was giving all he had. For a moment Vulpes felt the friendship he held for the plucky dog. He liked the old Red Bone, who never failed to accept his bold challenge for a race. Here was a hound that loved the chase.

Vulpes came to the edge of a big farm that lay on the other side of the road. An old rail fence bounded it. He leapt lightly to the top of the fence and ran swiftly along it, balancing himself with his tail. As he sped over the warm wood of the fence that had mellowed to a deep gray in the wind and rain and sun, he caught the movement of a brown body below him in the grass. Without any pause he pounced upon his unsuspecting prey. But it turned out to be a shrew, whose musty flavor didn't appeal to the fox, and Vulpes vaulted back on the fence. At a break in the rails he dropped to the ground again. The sun was warm and the sweet odor of the dry grasses enervated the fox. He rested on a bright hill as the long weeds moved gently above his head. Some of the stalks still held their seeds. The movement of his body against the grass sent the seeds drifting off to the fields.

Vulpes heard Brownie and Joe reach the fence. They had lost the trail again and were wearily seeking it in the brittle grasses and weeds. Joe was tired. His tongue hung from his mouth and his sides heaved heavily as he breathed. He was glad for the rest, for he was so weary he could hardly push on. He might never have found the trail again if it had not been for Brownie. The Red Bone would not give up. He knew that Vulpes was near-by. Nevertheless he searched easily, conserving himself until he could pick up the chase again. He worked back and forth, thinking that Vulpes might have jumped off the road again. When he was satisfied that he had not, he went back to the fence and smelt it carefully.

The fox watched the hounds for a moment and

then slipped through the field to a woodlot beyond. He was well rested now and set his course toward Sugar Loaf Mountain, miles away.

Brownie worried and worried around the fence post and then started down the field to see if Vulpes had crossed it anywhere. He ran right onto the spot where the fox had pounced on the shrew, just as Buck, Gordon and the three other hunters came striding out to River Road a quarter of a mile below.

Buck listened to his dogs.

"I believe that old red fox is heading over to Sugar Loaf," he said. "If he has, they won't be back until night."

Gordon looked at his watch. It was about 2:30. He was exhausted from the long tramp over the rough terrain and up and down the hills. He wondered if they were going to the mountain.

Brownie sounded the call of the hunt. Buck straightened up and listened.

"He's on it again!" But the hound did not repeat the cry. He could not tell where Vulpes had gone after he had found the shrew. It occurred to him, however, that the fence was the secret of the escape and he whined as he tried to jump up on it. Excitedly he ran down the field. Then Joe found the scent at the break in the fence. His glad baying called to the Red Bone and the hunters that the day was not done and that the fox might still be theirs.

With a crying howl the dogs followed the trail. Rested by the delay, the two hounds started off toward the mountains. While there was still a trail to follow the hounds would not give up. A farmer in the field below saw Vulpes cross his land. It was not long after that that he looked up from his hoe to see the gallant fox hounds tonguing along his trail.

Stacks turned to Buck Queen:

"Well, I guess we might as well go back and rest. Maybe we can pick up the chase in the morning."

"Yes," said old Buck. "There ain't any use following them now. They're off for the night." The five men shouldered their guns and walked down the long road to Buck's farm. It was late afternoon when they stomped the mud from their boots on the back porch and went into the parlor to talk over the chase.

Vulpes enjoyed the long stretch of farms, streams and woods on the way to Sugar Loaf Mountain. He led his pursuers over meadows and past brooks. He wound through groves of leafless trees and all afternoon the cry of dogs filled the lands behind him. From time to time he rested. Brownie had nearly reached him several times, but each time he had sprinted forward and left the hound far behind.

At dusk the fox crept along the forest at the foot of the mountain. The giant hill was dark and shadowy. A cold wind had blown up and was moaning through the formless treetops. Above the sad music of the wind, the fox could hear the constant voice of Brownie. It sounded weird and lonely.

Somewhere, during the night, the fox turned and led the dogs back toward the river. Vulpes, Brownie and Joe passed through the streets of small sleeping towns on the homeward lap. They loped by wooden churches with their white steeples high against the stars, and grocery stores that were guarded by sleeping cats. They crossed graveyards and slid under the iron fences into the empty gardens of roadside farmers. And a few heard them pass. A carpenter, tossing restlessly on his bed, thought he heard a plaintive cry coming from the mountains. A housewife awakened by her child wondered why the dogs were restless. The hunt went on.

Around three o'clock in the morning Vulpes came to Muddy Branch. He had raced the last four miles home and had left the dogs far behind. Deep in his protective woodlands he lay down to rest. The fox panted heavily and his eyes shone like glass goblets in the dark.

Then he heard the hounds closing in on him again. He rose and went on. Taking an old avenue, he went down to his homeland stream that wound under the beech and oaks. Dry leaves blew over the floor of the night woods. A cold wind moved up from the river, shaking the bare limbs of the trees. The fox was ready to lose the dogs for good.

About four in the morning he came to the canal. He waited. Far behind he heard them. They were still following, undaunted. Vulpes looked at the canal. A thin coat of ice had formed over the still waters. He judged the ice against his weight and then darted swiftly across the snapping surface.

Vulpes made the other bank with ease. He glided up the tow-path, retracing his steps of the day before.

Brownie was the first to reach the frozen waters. He could not catch the scent of the fox on the ice. But there was not a doubt in his mind but that he had crossed to the other side. Without hesitating, the hound sped onto the slippery surface and leapt to the far bank. As he sprang the ice broke under him. Brownie's feet were wet as he climbed the hill.

When Joe reached the canal, his companion was on the other side. His only thought was to clip the inside of the circle that Brownie had made to catch up with the hunt. Midway across the canal the thin surface broke beneath him. The sudden shock of the freezing water on his hot tired body knocked the breath from him. For a moment he was stunned. Then he lunged his chest against the ice and scrambled to regain his footing.

It was slow progress. The ice chipped as he paddled forward. When he placed his feet on the surface to pull himself out, it broke under the weight. Joe threw all his energy into one last spurt. He hit a solid chink of ice and strained forward. But the chilling effect of the water on his tired hot body had sapped his strength, and he could not quite make the last pull. Desperately he struggled, inching his body forward. Now his hind legs would not answer to his will. They trembled and refused to move. Joe clung to the solid ice with his fore paws as the cold began to shoot through his muscles. Then he felt his grip slipping. He sank slowly back into the water. The valiant hound disappeared beneath the quiet surface. Joe never came up again.

The water rippled away in growing circles where the hound had gone down. It lapped coldly against the ice. Small crystals began to seal over the break in the canal. Like silver darts they shot over the still waters glittering and sparkling as they grew, until gradually the little pocket was closed as if to seal away the woodland tragedy.

Joe had never given up the hunt. He had followed it until he could go no farther.

As the sun came up, Vulpes and Brownie were far up the canal. They crossed to the woodland side at the Seneca Locks and were running down toward Muddy Branch again when Buck awoke and went to the door.

He listened in the cold for a long time. Presently the voice of Brownie sounded faintly, barely audible in the distant hills. Buck returned to his warm parlor to dress. He was finishing his big plate of scrambled eggs as Will Stacks came up on the back porch. May opened the door for the trapper.

"Buck," Will said as he came in with a blast of

cold air, "the hounds are back. I heard 'em pass my place about two hours ago. I came over to see if you were going out again."

"I heard 'em, too," said Buck. "That is, I heard Brownie, not Joe."

Around eight o'clock Jim Gordon appeared.

"Are we going out again?" asked the young man eagerly. He had slept off the weariness of the previous day and was feeling fresh again.

"Yes," answered Buck, "I guess we'd better go out and see what's going on."

"Have they really been running all night?"

"Yes, indeed. Yes, indeed, they have! They've been clear over to Sugar Loaf and back. That fox will be cutting capers this morning. He won't want those dogs hanging on any longer."

The three men sat around the fire. Buck kept getting up and going to the door to listen.

"I don't hear Joe," he said, coming back. "Hope nothing's wrong."

Now Vulpes and Brownie were in the bottom lands below Buck's place. Vulpes passed the old goat pen and slipped through the page wire fence that marked off the property. Brownie was following. His ears flopped against his head. His feet felt heavier and heavier. He missed Joe now, but thought he had probably stopped to rest somewhere along the chase.

The hound came to the page fence and squeezed painfully through it. His body was thicker than Vulpes' and he could not leap through the tight mesh with the fox's ease. For several minutes he was held back by the barrier. With one last push he went squirming between the wires and sprawled onto the earth beyond.

Both animals were walking now. Vulpes had gone up a ravine. While he followed a ridge at the head of it, Brownie's voice rang out fitfully below him. As the day passed on, Brownie dropped farther and farther behind. The scent was becoming weak on the warming earth and the dog was feeling tired.

About noon Vulpes went up to River Road again. He paused at the side of the lane and looked down the long, rutted pike. In the distance around the bend he could hear a horse and wagon plodding along. The wagon was tossing and jostling as it rode the ditches and hard mud. Vulpes ran down the road. He had caught the scent of the load and knew what it was. The cart was full of manure. One of the farmers was driving it to the fields to dump. The fox didn't see the wagon as he trotted down the curving, hilly road before it. For several minutes he ran along far ahead of the load and then jumped off to the side of the road. The creaking wagon rolled over his trail as it plodded along. The rough road bounced the iron wheels and the manure flew into the air. The strong-scented pieces fell across his track. Vulpes scampered off into the woods and lay down at a safe distance to watch the next move of the Red Bone.

Meanwhile the hunters had gone out. They had picked up the bay of Brownie as he completed the circle around the hill and pushed up the ravine to River Road. Buck had two fresh young pups on leashes. He had brought them along to relieve the exhausted Brownie and Joe. The pups were wild and eager. It took all Buck's strength to hold them in.

Buck and his friends found the old Red Bone circling the road.

"Can't imagine where old Joe is," said Buck when he saw Brownie alone. The dog looked up at his master and wagged his tail. Then he dropped his head and tried to pick out the scent of the fox from the confusion of smells. He knew Vulpes was not far away. He was sure he could find his trail again.

Buck looked down and saw blotches of blood on the mud. The tired old dog had run the pads off his feet and was staining the earth as he ran. Still game to the hunt he pulled himself from one side of the road to the other with great effort. His master saw his trouble and set the young pups loose. They burst over to Brownie with a flash and tore wildly along the ground.

Brownie watched them out of bloodshot eyes. He knew they were not thinking out the search. They had no design to their work. He could not turn the hunt over to the careless pups. Brownie pushed forward. His swollen legs moved slowly.

Buck felt badly as he watched his gallant hound work. He knew he would continue the search until he dropped or found the trail. He wanted to take him out of the hunt, but the dog shied away from him and pressed his nose closer to the ground.

Then a deep throated bay came from his hoarse dry throat. Brownie had found the trail.

"He's worked it out! He's got that trail!" said Buck as he smiled fondly at his hound. No sooner had Brownie given voice than the young pups flocked over to him and burst off on Vulpes' trail.

Brownie stopped and watched them go. As he pushed forward to lead the pack, his feet dragged and pains shot through his stiff muscles. Holding his nose high he loped forward. Then Brownie collapsed. He could go no farther. Buck rushed to his side and leaned over him. He picked up his feverish head and stroked it, working his strong fingers over his muscles to keep them from growing stiff. Brownie

looked up at the old hunter from his sad hound eyes. He flopped his tail against the ground.

Buck took off his heavy sweater. He wrapped the hound in the warm knitted wool and gently picked him up.

Jim Gordon had been standing a few feet away, watching the scene without saying a word. He was struck by the ferocity and intensity of the hunt, reflected in the noble dog who even though battered and exhausted still wanted to follow it. Brownie's ears lifted anxiously when the baying of the young hounds rang back through the woods. But the spent Red Bone could not even muster enough energy to attempt a struggle to free himself from Buck's arms. He could only whimper without moving as the men started back to the hunter's home.

Back at the farm the old hunter carefully put the dog in his kennel. He wrapped an old burlap bag around him to keep the cold from his trembling body. He brought him food and water and rubbed him briskly to restore some tone to his flagging muscles.

Brownie did not move all day or the next night. He was completely exhausted. Around noon the next day he put his head out of his door to eat, but he didn't rise until another night had passed.

The fox rested while the dogs worked out the trail. When he was ready to move on he rose and glided swiftly to the glen below. He walked up the next hill. Vulpes was tired. He wanted to go back to Muddy Branch and Fulva. He wanted to sleep.

Suddenly he heard the baying of the pups. Their voices rang out with freshness and pep across the countryside. The fox darted onward. Here was new energy. He raced down through the woods and out of earshot of the hounds. He knew he must trick them soon or they might corner him before he reached his haven. The fox gave one powerful leap and jumped far to the right of the trail. He cleared nearly six yards in a last effort to lose the hunt. Trotting swiftly he darted up the hill to an old trail that circled back to the stream in the bottomlands.

For once the hounds behaved as the fox had

planned. The young dogs overshot the trail in their eagerness and soon lost the fox. They circled excitedly, wondering what to do next. Their fresh enthusiasm and abounding youthful energies carried them crashing through the thickets, but away from their quarry. The hunt was done.

Buck sat down quietly to his dinner that night. Several times he interrupted his meal to go to the door and look for Joe. He came back each time with a worried expression on his face.

"I don't understand why that hound isn't back, May," he said slowly. "It's not like him. I'm afraid something has happened to that dog."

Will Stacks went back to his shack along River Road. He thought about the hunt and Vulpes as he drove along.

"Still didn't get that old prince," he murmured. "Still can't outwit him." Somehow he felt that no one ever would.

Jim Gordon stretched out on the bunk in his farmhouse. He was too tired to get up and prepare supper. He smiled to himself as he thought that a slim little fox had worn him out. Gordon dropped to sleep thinking of the clever animal that had outdone them all.

The next morning he went over to Buck's to inquire about Joe and Brownie.

The old Red Bone had not moved from his spot. Buck was gone when Gordon knocked at the door.

"He's out hunting for Joe," May said. "He is sure something happened to that dog and it kind of knocked the spirits out of him."

"Which way did he go?" Gordon asked. May pointed down the road and the young man strode off to help in the search.

Vulpes had returned to the laurel slick and slept away the night. He had not even looked for food. At

dawn he skirted the nearby woods for mice and rabbits. He heard Fulva running along the stream toward the river. For several minutes he listened to her light feet flying along the leaves. Then he turned away from Muddy Branch and left the area. Vulpes returned to his early homeland. He had enough of the hunt.

He did not wait for Fulva. It was early winter and he was willing to spend the next few months by himself. Later he would come back to her again. Now, however, he wanted to be alone and free in the winter hills. His resilient muscles carried him effortlessly away.

CHAPTER ELEVEN

Years later the people of the Potomac still talked of the big hunt. Some retold the stories that Buck Queen and Will Stacks had told and elaborated on the events. Others said they had seen Vulpes at night wandering along the farm stealing chickens and pigs and lambs. Others said that they had heard him call at night and that his voice resounded from mountain to mountain. Many were the tall tales about Vulpes, the Red Fox. He had become famous, and it was reported by those who had never seen a fox that he was as big as a setter and wild as a timber wolf.

But Vulpes had spent these years quietly in the Muddy Branch region. He returned to his favorite haunt each spring to seek Fulva and they had raised many families in the seclusion of the glades and beech trees. Little disturbed his life after the big hunt and but for casual races with the young pups, Vulpes had no real challenging sport.

For Brownie had dropped from the hunts after the now famous thirty-six-hour chase. Buck knew that his dog was no longer equal to the demands of the fox hunt, so he used Brownie for night work on coons and possums.

One night Buck was out in the woods with Brownie after a coon whose tracks he had noticed down in the flats that day. Brownie still had his keen nose and quick instincts and did not need his old endurance on these hunts.

Buck and Brownie followed the road leading to the flats and turned off below the gate that enclosed the next property. They started up a hill, the dog working through the area they were covering to find the coon. Suddenly the hound hit Vulpes' trail. He bayed and started off in pursuit. Buck called to him and he circled back reluctantly and made an effort to trail the coon. But his love of the hunt was too great. He started off on Vulpes' scent once more and wound down through the woods. Buck called, and then stopped to listen. He was sure it was Vulpes that Brownie was chasing for the old hunter understood his hound perfectly. Buck turned to retrace his steps as he heard the baying of the Red Bone die away in the hills. The dog would do this only when alone. If he were with a pack he would never have attempted the chase because he could no longer lead. He had spent himself on the big hunt. Buck left the hound and the red fox to their woodland paths and wandered slowly home, the thrilling sound of the hunt ringing softly far away.

Vulpes heard Brownie while stalking a rabbit in a field. He stood still and his ears twitched forward. The strong giant fox, now in the prime of his years, turned his head in the direction of the baying. He knew it was Brownie and that he had come trailing him through the woods for the love of the chase. The great fox waited and then started out slowly to lead his friend down the hills and over the glades of their youth.

The hound was lumbering along puffing hard on the hills and rushing down them in such a way that he caught his breath. Vulpes remembered their old games and he waded shallow streams for a few yards to give the dog a rest and to challenge him with their old sports. Brownie worked out each puzzle quickly, for he knew just what the fox would do. For several hours they played, Vulpes crossing fallen trees, Brownie picking up his trail on the other side, Vulpes backtracking on his trail, Brownie finding the spot where he had vaulted to one side. Then the dog felt his age and the old pains shot through his legs again. He slowed down and finally came to a stop. With a last resounding bay, he turned to go home.

Vulpes heard him give up the hunt and ran back over his trail to the knoll of the hill where he could see the dark shadow of the Red Bone limping off through the woods. He put his head down and barked his slurring yap. Brownie halted to look back a moment, but then moved on. The fox came a few yards closer and sat down in the leaves. He watched the hound until he disappeared in the night, and his scent was carried off by the wind.

Vulpes got up and resumed his search for food.

Brownie came up to Buck's door about an hour after the old hunter had fallen asleep and barked as he had always done when returning from a fox hunt. Buck had dropped off to sleep in his big chair by the fire, waiting for his dog to come home. He came out and patted his head. Brownie's food was ready and Buck led the dog back to his kennel. As they went, Brownie lifted his head high as he passed the kennels of the younger dogs who had been awakened by the commotion and had stepped from their doors to inquire into the reason.

"Good old Brownie," Buck said as he tied the dog to his leash. "You love to run that fellow, don't you? 'Deed you do, Brownie, 'deed you do."

The next night Will Stacks came by to visit Buck.

He brushed his feet clean on the doormat and walked out of the cold night into the warm kitchen.

"Good evening, May," he said as he dropped his coat on a chair.

"Good evening, Will. Go right in. Buck is in by the stove." The two men took seats by the fire and puffed away on their pipes in silence.

"Heard from that big old red fox last night," Buck began.

"Is that so? I reckon he'll be around for a long time. I still haven't been able to set a trap that'll fool him."

"Old Brownie got him up," Buck went on, pursuing his own trend of thought. "Yep, he got up a fox, and just as sure as I'm alive it was that old Vulpes we chased on the big hunt. Brownie lit out after him like I haven't seen him do in years."

Will sat quietly thinking of the beautiful wild creature that had figured so deeply in the lives of the men.

"Noticed a lot of gray foxes lately," said Buck. "Seem to be coming in in big numbers the last year or so."

"I've noticed that myself," the trapper agreed. "Get an awful lot of them. So many I'm wondering if it's worth trapping any more. Getting old, I guess,

but it seems like too much trouble to take just to get a gray fox."

"Wonder what the reason is?" asked Buck.

"Well, I don't know, but it may be that a lot of these wealthy city people buying up the woodlots and moving in has something to do with it. That's the red fox's territory, you know, and people living right on top of 'em doesn't please 'em any. They aren't buying those old wet bottoms where the gray fox lives, and I guess that's why they're getting by better."

"Well, that just might be right," said Buck after a pause, "but I don't know. We just don't know all the answers, do we, Will?"

"Sure don't."

"I hear Charlie is right bad off. A very old and feeble man now. All the old fellows are gone except you and me, Will."

"Yes. Well, I guess we're still a match for most of 'em. I'll bet we could still outwalk that young Gordon on a hunt."

"I would like to get hold of one more good dog man," said Buck, thinking about the hunt. "I want to raise me some more good hounds. One more like old Brownie or old Joe and we could get that red fox."

"Did I tell you about the time I tracked Vulpes?" Will asked.

"Don't remember that you did."

"I've been tracking him in the snow. I've been doing that a good bit, Buck. Want to find out all I can about that old dog fox. Figure if I learn that one, I'll be able to match the best of 'em."

"Tracks in the snow sure tell the story, Will."

"I jumped him one day after following his foot-steps for about a mile. He had checked each squirrel digging, investigated each burrow and tuft of grass. He sure is a thorough-going critter. He doesn't miss a trick. Then, all of a sudden, I stirred him from a sleep in that old laurel thicket near Muddy Branch and he glided out of there just like an arrow. Well, I tracked him a while longer and then turned to go home.

"Soon I noticed fox tracks alongside my footsteps that I had left while going the other way. And do you know, Buck, that old fox was trailing me while I was trailing him! I don't think I would have ever caught him."

"That's a clever animal, Will. He sure is a cun-ning thing."

Buck was laughing pleasantly when a knock at the door aroused the two men. They heard May wel-come Jim Gordon.

"Evening, Mr. Gordon. How's that boy of yours?"

"He's fine, big enough so that I can come out to the farm and bring him along," smiled Jim. "It will be nice to have more time out here again." Jim sat down with the other men. He had married since the big hunt, and had not been on a chase since that one several years before. However, Gordon had made use of the experience and had told the story of Vulpes, the Red Fox, over and over to his friends, enlarging it word by word until some listeners thought the whole story was fiction.

"Remember that old . . ."

"Vulpes?" finished Stacks. "Sure do. See him every now and then."

"Do you think we could try once more to get him?" the young man asked.

"Well now, we just might do that," Buck said. "The dogs I've got are getting to be right good hunters. Not the equal of Brownie or Joe, but they've learned a lot and are fairly good hounds, particularly that young Billy Sunday hound, Trigger."

"I sure would like to go out," Gordon said.

Vulpes stirred, then he dropped easily to the ground and stretched his muscles. He had been curled up on a dry bed of needles carpeting a rock slab beneath a scrub pine. The pine grew on a rugged bluff overlooking Muddy Branch. Just what awakened him is hard to say. With the caution that made him famous he always slept lightly. His naps were frequent but irregular and short. Roused from his slumbers, he found he was hungry and had automatically taken up the search for food without further thought. Even as he dropped from the rock his keen nose was testing the air for scents of possible food or danger. His wants were few and simple and his action direct. He set out immediately and trotted silently down the hill to cross the stream on the aqueduct where it flowed beneath the canal. On the other side he set his course to work upwind toward the farmlands. His zig-zag track carried him to every spot his alert senses detected as possible sources of food. As he moved, his ears picked up the sounds on either side, his nose told him what to expect far ahead, and his eyes told him the way. He realized he was not alone.

The night woods seemed filled with hunters. Vison, the mink, scouted the stream with a relentless fury that sent chills of terror through his hapless victims. Procyon, the raccoon, watched from his retreat in a hollow tree. After Vulpes had passed beneath him, the inquisitive Procyon descended to the ground and followed him toward the farms. Near the margin of the woods Vulpes caught the musky odor of Mephitis, the skunk. Mephitis was moving slowly and deliberately across an old abandoned orchard, stopping to dig and root in the sod every now and then. Few animals bothered the skunk and he moved without fear.

Tamias, the chipmunk, and Marmota, the wood-chuck, were hibernating in their burrows, but most of the animals were active. Vulpes played his part in this activity. Each was intent on securing his own food or prey. This was the normal cycle of the wild. Hunters and hunted, food or prey. Some must perish that others might live. Some found food in plants. The carnivores lived upon the herbivores; and so the cycle went on. Those best able to cope with the world they lived in and satisfy their simple demands, survived.

For the present, Vulpes was the hunter; perhaps in the morning he would become the hunted.

The night was cool, quiet and pleasant with the melody of tragedy that always hung over the woodland, coloring the scene with sad beauty. The moon rose to spread its yellow light across the white snows, leaving black linear shadows that raced across the woodland as the clouds blew along the heavens. As the moon rose higher in the skies the jet-black velvet of the heavens with its sparkling blue-white stars, paled before it.

A heavy blanket of snow dampened all sounds. No leaves were free to rattle across the woodland floor. The snow lay on the tangled mats of the dormant honeysuckle and weighed the vines down. The thick white cloak made grotesque figures that stood motionless on the woodland floor. Black pools of water at the foot of snow-rimmed falls in the tiny streams heightened the effect of the ghost-like forest. This was the woodland of the wild. So unlike the same woodlot during the day. When the protection of the vale of darkness hung over it, the wild creatures of the woods came out from their hiding places to carry on their life. At night the woods became a primeval forest.

Vulpes moved to the fence line that marked the farm land border. Here in the old and long-ago-abandoned orchard he caught a mouse. He kept on until he had caught a rabbit. His hunger satisfied, he returned to his lair and fell asleep.

"Oroowoooooo, oroowoooooo, oroowooo, oroowoo uoo," and Vulpes knew the hounds were after him. He roused himself from his slumber and walked through the woods ahead of the chase. The clean air filled his lungs and the fox pranced as he wound through the trees, glad that the winter sports were beginning again and that the hunts were on.

Vulpes loved these days, but he was never unaware of the threat of the hunter and his gun. Too often he had heard the report of the shotgun blast its way through the trees to know that this was not all pleasure. But though at times he felt uneasy during the hunt, his knowledge gained on past hunts gave him confidence. He knew the trails Buck Queen took even as Buck Queen knew his. He knew that when Buck brought his friends he would station them throughout the woods and then it was time for him to leave.

He thought he would circle down to Muddy Branch and possibly lead the hounds off toward Sugar Loaf.

"Oroowoo, orouwooooo," the baying of the

hounds sounded nearer. Vulpes looked up at the wind-filled sky that sparkled through the limbs of the trees and turned to wind through the valleys.

Buck had placed Will Stacks and Jim Gordon at stations that were along the probable route of the fox.

After he had turned the dogs loose early that morning, he had climbed into his car with Stacks and Gordon and had started down River Road to Muddy Branch. When they came to the ford where the creek crossed the pike, the hunters parked the car, and followed an old logging trail through the woods. The three of them had walked silently up a creek bed after turning off the road and Buck had placed his two friends.

He went alone to find his own station. He carried his gun slung through his arm and walked swiftly. Buck passed through a low valley that had been cut out by a stream. He came onto a large flat pocket rimmed by four hills that rose above it. The pocket glade was open and Buck could see much of the woodland floor. A dense patch of laurel covered one of the hills and blotted its earthen base from view. The hills above him were canopied with tall straight trees that stood in the hollow. It created a natural amphitheater.

Buck left the stream and took his stand by a white oak a few feet from the water. It was a tall slender tree, only about a dozen inches wide. Buck leaned against the gray bark. He set his gun in front of the tree where he could easily reach it. His left thumb was hooked in a ragged buttonhole of his coat. His hat was pushed back from his head, and he watched the valleys like a hawk. He was part of the tree, so silently he stood. Only the searching turn of his head belied his presence.

A quiet hush settled over the valley while Buck waited. A red-shouldered hawk swooped over the top of the trees and took his perch high above the glade. From here he surveyed the woods around him. The hawk had hardly settled himself before a party of blue jays saw him and came screaming through

the trees to attack the giant bird. Their annoying chatter and fussing and their persistent diving attacks forced the good-natured Buteo to leave his perch. He lifted himself off the limb tops, drifted out into the wind and circled away.

A moment after the blue jays had bullied the hawk into leaving, they darted over the hill and set up their chatter beyond the hollow. Buck watched them carefully. He listened closely as they went through the tree branches across the crest of the hill. Then he noticed that they were directing their attacks at something on the ground.

He could not see what it was but he closed his fingers around his gun.

They fussed around the far edge of the laurel patch for some minutes, then lost interest and flew off toward the fields and farms beyond.

Buck noted all these details very closely, for his life in the open had taught him to be observant. Noting things like this and threading them into the pattern of the woods and the wildlife that lived there was compensation enough in itself for Buck. He was happy just to spend a day in these surroundings with the anticipation that comes with the hunt. Even if he brought home no game he did not care. Hunting in the manner in which he did it was a sportsman-like way and was only possible to those like himself who were students of the woods and fields. While he stood motionless, contemplating the meaning of the screaming jays, he wondered if it might be a fox.

Vulpes was traveling far ahead of the hounds and was circling the crest of a hill when the jays came screaming through the treetops. He quickly darted into a heavy cover of laurel and there was hidden from sight. The jays soon lost interest and flew away. He went on down the hill and through the laurel thicket.

At the edge of the thicket he paused and sniffed the air. There were no forbidding smells. He was fully alerted to the hunt, and alive to its dangers.

His senses were keyed to the highest pitch. While his nose tasted the breeze at the end of the thicket, he realized that he was going downwind and appreciated the dangers that that entailed. He decided to go down the hill, cross the creek and circle back upwind.

Buck Queen saw the fox leave the thicket only two hundred yards across the hollow. His pulse quickened as he recognized Vulpes. He mused to himself:

"He *is* a beautiful thing!"

He didn't move as he watched the fox draw closer.

Vulpes slipped smoothly from the protection of the laurel leaves and glided down to the stream bed. He followed the high bank to a point where he could leap the brook. The ground was cool under his feet, and the earth smelt of the warm body of Blarina, who was working off on the hill somewhere, eagerly hunting insect grubs for his food.

Running downwind, Vulpes' keen nose betrayed him. Although his eyes were sharp, he noticed nothing in the quiet woods until Buck put out his left hand and picked up his gun. Vulpes caught this movement even as it began and swerved immediately to gather himself for a tremendous leap across the stream.

Buck raised his gun and trained it on the flying red form. The sharp report echoed through the hollows and faded away in the valleys.

Buck never missed.

The hunt was done.

About the Author

Since this book was originally published, Jean Craighead George has written many more, among them *Julie of the Wolves*, which was awarded the Newbery Medal in 1973. *My Side of the Mountain* was a Newbery Honor Book, an ALA Notable Book, and a Hans Christian Andersen Award Honor Book, and was made into a major motion picture. Both *My Side of the Mountain* and its sequel, *On the Far Side of the Mountain*, are available in Puffin editions. Jean Craighead George lives in Chappaqua, New York.